Venus in Twilight

a love story

J P McAndrew

First edition July 2023, Infinity Heart Press.

Dedication

To my coworker Paul, whose interesting marriage inspired this story. You came up with a beautiful solution to an impossible problem.

To my beta readers, especially MB Strang, Denis McBee, Bill Phillips, and Kim Vogel, for your valuable advice, feedback, and encouragement.

To the reader on Wattpad who messaged, "OMG! I didn't want it to end!" That came at a good time. I really needed it.

To my children Nick and Sya.

But most of all to Kimberly Lucia Della Mia Vita, light of my life.

Chapter 1

THE CANDIDATE

Life can turn on a dime.

Madison was reminded of this as she tried to find her Lexus in the hotel parking lot.

It was gone.

"No!"

She turned slowly, scanning the cars to be sure, but she knew she wouldn't find it. She clearly remembered parking it next to the lamp post right *there*, and now in its place was a red Mustang.

She stomped the pavement.

She clenched her fists and yelled at the sky. "Fuck!"

She felt a panic attack coming on. She doubled over and put her hands on her knees until she could catch her breath. She stood and looked at her phone, trying to decide whether to call a taxi or Uber. She groaned. There wasn't time.

Fucking Lars!

She called his number, fighting back tears as she crossed the parking lot.

"You piece of shit!" she yelled.

She got his voicemail greeting.

"This is Lars Lundquist, guitarist and metal god. I can't come to the phone right now. Please leave a message." Beep.

She crossed the busy avenue, faced the oncoming traffic, and stuck out her thumb.

"I need my car! I need it right now! I know you took it! You'd better bring it back A-S-A-P, or I'm calling the police!"

She ended the call and stuck the phone in her purse.

A dozen vehicles passed her. One slowed, the window down, and the driver yelled, "Hey, baby!" but he didn't stop.

She turned and gave him the finger.

More cars passed. She was running out of time. But a silver Buick slowed, then stopped on the shoulder with its emergency flashers on. She ran to the passenger's side and looked into the open window.

The driver looked back. He was about 40, with glasses and graying hair.

"I'm trying to decide if you're safe," she said.

"I don't blame you," he said.

"I'm desperate."

"Okay. Hop in."

She opened the door and slid into the passenger's seat.

"I've never hitched before," she said as the man eased the car back onto the road.

"I've never picked anyone up before. Where are you going?"

"Do you know Commerce Park?"

"Yeah, that's where I work. I can take you right there."

Lucky break. The Fates were toying with her, but maybe this day wouldn't be so bad.

"You know hitch-hiking is dangerous, right?" the man said.

"Yeah, but how many serial killers snag their victims at eight-thirty in the morning?"

"Beats me. I don't know any serial killers," he said.

"Anyway, I Had to take the chance. My car's been stolen."

"That sucks. Did you make a police report?"

"Didn't have time. I have a job interview. And there's a chance the car will come back."

"That literally never happens."

"It might this time. I used to be married to the prime suspect. He's done this before."

The man didn't say anything for a moment. He said, "Wow."

"My name's Madison."

"Alex," he said. "Where's the interview? I know a few of the neighbors."

"It's called Tucker-Herman. Have you heard of them?"

"Why, yes." His expression was cryptic.

"What have you heard?" she asked.

"I've heard that it's a great place to work, but the owners are a couple of assholes. Especially Brad Tucker."

"Really?" She frowned.

"That's what I've heard. And here we are."

He entered the complex and parked in front of a small office building.

She took a deep breath. "How's my hair?"

"Fine. You look good."

"Okay. Here we go."

"Good luck."

"Thanks. You saved my life."

She looked at her watch as she walked to the door. Ten minutes early.

•♥•♥•♥•♥•♥•

Inside the entrance of the office suite, she found a well-appointed lounge without a receptionist. She found a coffee maker and poured herself a cup. She sat, sipped coffee, and tried to calm her jangled nerves. After a few minutes, a man came around the corner. She stood. His appearance said "tech entrepreneur chic": a goatee, blazer, dress shirt open at the collar, jeans, and sneakers:

"Madison Lundquist?" he asked.

"Yes." She extended her hand, and he shook it.

"Brad Tucker. Right this way."

He led her down the hallway to an office. The door was open, and he gestured for her to enter. "Take a seat." He pulled out a cell phone and spoke. "I'm interviewing a candidate. I'd like you to be here." And to Madison: "My partner will be right in. Before we begin, do you have any questions?"

"I've learned some things about you from your website, mostly. Which is terrific, by the way."

"Of course. That's what we do."

"You have a good reputation and some big clients. Any plans for growth?"

Brad smiled. "That's why you're here. We've grown to the point where I can't handle all the sales calls by myself. I'd like to cut back to sixteen-hour days."

The man they were waiting for entered—Alex, who had given her the lift. Her eyes widened. It was awkward.

"This is my partner, Alex Herman," Brad said. Brad noticed her dismay. "What?"

"Surprise!" Alex said. "I picked her up on the way to work. Her car's been stolen." He took a seat by the wall.

"Well, that's too bad," Brad said.

"He didn't tell me who he was." Madison laughed. "He said Tucker-Herman was run by a couple of assholes. Funny."

"It's true. I can be an asshole sometimes," Brad said.

"What about Mr. Herman?" Madison asked.

"He's an asshole all of the time."

Alex laughed.

Brad started the formal interview. He asked the questions while Alex observed. They reviewed Madison's education: the BS in Psychology at the University of Wisconsin, main campus; graduate work in Marketing at Eau Claire. No master's yet, but hopefully, that was in the cards. Work history: ad sales for several newspapers in the midwest, a radio station in Des Moines, and finally, the ABC affiliate tv station in LA.

"Why did you go into sales?" he asked.

"Because I'm really good at it," she said.

Brad nodded, then asked one last question. "I know it's a cliche, but I have to ask: where do you see yourself in ten years?"

She said, "Right here, if the work is rewarding."

Brad looked at her closely. "Okay. Give us a couple of days to interview the other candidates. We'll get back to you on Wednesday."

They all stood.

"Do you mind if I stay and meet your staff?" Madison asked. "I'd like to make sure this is a good fit. I promise not to get in the way."

Brad looked surprised but pleased. He'd probably never had a candidate make that request. He pulled out his phone.

"Are you busy?" he asked the person on the other end. "Do you have time to give a tour and make introductions?" He put the phone away. "Lilith will meet you in the lounge," he told Madison.

"I have work to do," Alex said. He extended his hand to Madison, and they shook again. "Welcome aboard," he said softly.

"See you later, asshole," said Brad.

Alex chuckled as he left the office.

Madison found her way back to the lounge, where she was met by a willowy young woman wearing a Goth-inspired ensemble. Eccentric, but the young woman wore it like a business suit.

"You must be Madison. I'm Lilith, graphic design. Come on. I'll show you around."

Lilith took her to the break room and showed her the restrooms, the conference room, and a block of offices. It seemed as though Alex and Brad were the only occupants.

"Where is everyone?" Madison asked.

"You'll see." Lilith led her to the end of the hall. "We call this 'the pit.'" She opened the door to the room at the end. Inside were eight or ten young men and women staring at monitors, clicking at keyboards.

"This room was set up for the programmers, but we all get along pretty well, so we spend a lot of time here. If anyone needs some quiet time, they can go to their private space. Best of both worlds. Hey, everyone! This is Madison." Everyone swiveled in their office chairs to face the door.

"Hi, Madison," said one man about Madison's age.

"That's Garth," Lilith said. "He's our senior programmer. And next to him is Bob."

"Junior programmer," Garth said.

"Get over yourself," Bob replied. "Madison, what do you play?"

She was puzzled. "Why? Are you starting a band?"

They all laughed.

"We're all gamers here."

"Oh, of course. Minecraft, Fortnight."

Bob said, "We'll get you into some edgier stuff."

"We'll see. I haven't been hired yet."

"That's strange," Garth said. "Brad never gives a tour unless it's a done deal."

Lilith smiled. "I've got a good feeling."

Madison stuck around the pit and made herself comfortable. She sipped coffee and listened to the banter, mainly good-natured ribbing, like that of siblings.

She could see herself working here.

At lunchtime, they abandoned their computers one by one and went to the break room. She bought a tuna sandwich from a vending machine. Alex sat at a picnic table outside, eating something from a casserole dish. She opened the door.

"Mind if I join you?" she asked.

He looked up.

"Not at all," he said. "What do you think?"

"It'll do. If I get the job."

"You will. All the other candidates have sales experience, but not in advertising. That's a whole different animal. And you did great in the interview."

"You've got a twisted sense of humor, Mr. Herman."

"Call me Alex. I just wanted to see how you'd react."

"How'd I do?"

"You handled yourself like a pro. Let me know when you're ready to go. I'll take you back to the hotel."

"I can get an Uber. I wouldn't want to put you out."

"It's on my way. I can finish what I have to do at home."

"Thanks. This day would've been a disaster if you hadn't come along."

She returned to the pit and stayed until after two, and then her anxiety got the better of her. She had to get her car back. She dreaded the showdown with Lars.

She found Alex's office and tapped on the open door's frame.

"Ready?" he asked.

"Yep," she said.

He closed his laptop, put it in a bag, and joined her at the door.

When they pulled into the hotel parking lot, her Lexus had returned, two spaces from where she had left it.

"There it is," she said.

"I'll be damned." His brow furrowed. "Why would your ex do that?"

She shrugged. "Why does he do anything?"

"He must have spare keys."

"He said he lost them. Must've found them again. How did he know where I'd be? I haven't talked to him in months."

"Do you think he was following you?"

She laughed. "Not the way I drive."

"Tracking software on your phone?"

She shook her head. "Got a new phone after we split up."

"Then he put a tracking device on your car."

"I don't think he's that smart."

Alex fiddled with his phone. "Checking for Bluetooth devices," he explained. "It's just a hunch." After a minute, he got out and walked to the Lexus, looking at the phone. Madison followed. He got down on his hands and knees and looked under the rear bumper. Nothing. He felt under the left rear wheel well, then the left front.

"Here," he said. He pulled out a small, round device, a bit larger than a quarter, glued to a magnet.

"That son of a bitch," she said.

"It's a new thing. They make it easy to stalk people these days." He gave her a stern look. "You should go to another hotel until you find something more permanent."

She agreed. Alex took the tracking device and stuck it to a nearby light pole.

"He'll think you're still here." He handed her a business card. "Call me if you need anything."

"I will."

He got into his car and headed home.

She checked out of the hotel and found a room on the other side of town.

She left a message for Lars on his voicemail: she didn't appreciate being stalked and having her car stolen. She demanded he return the spare keys. He called back the next morning, and they arranged to meet in public, at the Olive Garden on State Street.

She parked the Lexus at the shopping mall a quarter mile away. She didn't want to give Lars a chance to plant another tracking device.

Lars walked in forty minutes late. He looked haggard and malnourished. His long blond hair was dirty. The charisma he used to have was gone. He wasn't the guy she'd married anymore. It was sad.

"You're late," she said.

“It took me a while to find the place.”

“Really? Because it’s literally right across the street from where you stole the Lexus last night.”

“I only borrowed it.”

“I almost missed a job interview because of you.” She held out her hand. He produced the keys and dropped them into her palm. “Do you owe money to someone?”

“The club owner stiffed us on our last gig. I needed some...things.”

“So you used my car as collateral for a loan.” For drugs, no doubt.

“*Our* car. My name’s on the title, too.”

“Not anymore. You’re lucky I didn’t call the police.”

He glared at her. “Why are you being such a bitch?”

The waitress came with a menu for Lars. “Can I get you anything?”

“Yeah,” Madison threw her napkin at Lars. “I’d like a restraining order for this dipshit.” She stood and made for the door.

She walked outside and toward the shopping mall. She found the pepper spray in her bag and got it ready, just in case. She was halfway to the mall when, sure enough, she spotted Lars’s junker out of the corner of her eye. She entered the mall at the entrance by California Pizza. The mall had too many doors for Lars to predict where she’d go out. She exited at the south JC Penney entrance, where her car was parked. She looked around. Lars was nowhere to be seen.

The next day, she was anxious. She exercised and showered, which helped. She ate breakfast in the hotel restaurant. She checked google maps to get the lay of this new town she might be calling home. She took a nap, swam, and watched tv when evening came.

Wednesday morning, her phone rang from a number that wasn't on her contact list.

"This is Madison."

"Brad Tucker here. Congratulations. You got the job. Can you be here tomorrow at nine?"

Over the next few weeks, she settled in nicely. Brad took her along on his sales calls. The idea was that if she worked out, and once she got comfortable, she would handle the smaller clients, allowing Brad to focus his charm and energy on the big money accounts. But for now, they went out as a team. She shadowed him for the first two weeks, acted as his assistant, and observed. In her second two weeks, she handled clients while Brad watched and gave her feedback.

Her first impression of Brad was that he was arrogant, but she grew to like him. He was intelligent and charismatic. She had mistaken his confidence for arrogance.

Alex supervised the programmers and kept to himself, so she had less contact with him. Her first impression of him was that he was sophisticated and aloof, like James Bond. That first impression also proved to be wrong.

Lilith was eccentric. She had an interest in ancient religions and led a Neo-Pagan worship group. She was a vegetarian and practiced yoga. She was exactly the kind of quirky individual that Madison was drawn to. They quickly became close friends.

Madison got to know the rest of her coworkers—four programmers, another graphic designer, two copywriters, and a woman specializing in animation and audio. Everyone at Tucker-Herman was brilliant because Brad only hired the best.

She learned what kind of take-out they ordered, who they were dating, which online games they played, and what music they liked. She became comfortable, and happier than she had been in a long time. Tucker-Herman started to feel like family.

She was going to be okay.

Chapter 2

MEET THE NEIGHBORS

Lucy's boobs strained against the fabric of her t-shirt as if they were trying to escape. That was the first thing Alex saw when he woke—not a bad way to start the day.

It was the Saturday before Memorial Day. It had gotten warm overnight, and the bedding lay in a pile at the foot of the bed.

Lucy slept on her side, facing him. The t-shirt was at least ten years old and threadbare. It was her favorite shirt for sleeping because it was soft and comfortable. The hem was hiked up above her hips.

It would have been nice to make love to her, but she liked her sleep. She wouldn't appreciate being awakened for sex.

He enjoyed the view until he felt his privates tingle.

"Down, boy," he whispered. "Maybe we'll get lucky later."

Lucy moaned. "Who are you talking to?" she asked.

"Myself," he said.

"Are you getting up?"

"You could say that."

"Gonna sleep a while longer."

"Okeedokee."

He kissed her on the head and rolled out of bed.

He made a cup of coffee, powered up the laptop computer in the breakfast nook, and went through his email. He had finished the first cup when he heard the roar of a truck. Gears ground and brakes squeaked as it turned into the crescent drive of the house next door. The top of a yellow moving van inched along above the tall hedges. Truck doors squeaked open and banged closed. The moving crew chattered as they rolled up the truck's rear door and slid out a metal ramp.

He stepped out the front door and onto the lawn to observe. A half-dozen young men dressed in coveralls carried boxes and furniture into the house.

He watched for a moment, then returned to his work in the breakfast nook. The toilet flushed upstairs in the master bath. He got a cup of coffee ready for Lucy. He heard her making her way down the stairs.

"Good morning," he said when she came into the kitchen. "How'd you sleep?"

"Like a log, until that racket started."

She sat across from him.

"The new neighbors," he said. He handed her a medicine bottle. "Prozac," he said. He set her coffee mug in front of her. "And vitamin C."

"I hope they like us." She took one of the capsules and popped it into her mouth. She washed it down with coffee. "Do you think they'll be as nice as the Rossettis?"

"We'll find out pretty soon."

"I should make them something. Brownies?"

"Sounds good," he said. "Brownies will be fine. I've got work to do." He closed the laptop, kissed her on the head, and went downstairs to his office in the basement.

A couple of hours later, the smell of brownies wafted down.

Lucy called to him: "Almost ready. I'm hopping in the shower."

"I'll be right there."

He finished his work and put the computer to sleep. When he got to the bedroom, Lucy was drying herself off. Alex brushed his teeth and showered as well. When he got out, Lucy was already dressed.

"Let's bust a move," she said. "Time's wastin'."

"Wow, you're excited," he said as he pulled on his jeans.

"It's not every day you get new neighbors."

By the time he was dressed, Lucy had her platter of brownies wrapped in saran and was waiting by the door like a racehorse at the starting gate.

"Okay, okay. Let's go."

They went outside and headed across the lawn.

"I miss the Rossettis," Lucy said.

"Things change. You have to adapt."

The moving crew was finishing up. A tall, affable man in his seventies stood back and watched them.

Alex stuck out his hand. "You must be Frank Holloway."

"Yes," said Frank as he gave Alex a firm handshake.

"Welcome to the neighborhood. Alex Herman. This is my wife, Lucy."

"I made brownies," said Lucy as she presented the platter.

"Thank you! They look delicious!" He took the platter from her. "Come inside and meet the old lady."

Frank led them into the house. It was chaos, filled with furniture and stacks of moving boxes. Frank led them to the kitchen, where a petite redhead was putting things away. She was much younger than Frank, about their age. Alex assumed it was Frank's daughter. He was wrong.

"There's the old girl now," Frank said. Alex and Lucy could barely contain their surprise. Frank looked amused. "Sweetie, these are the Hermans, Alex and Lucy. This is my wife, Kori tis Thelassis Holloway."

"Wow! That's a mouthful," Lucy said.

"I know!" said the woman. "Call me Kay."

She came in without warning and hugged Lucy, then Alex. She released him and stepped back.

"Look at them, Frank!" Kay said. "Aren't they the cutest? I think I'm going to like being neighbors with you two."

"We'll let you settle in," Alex said. "We just wanted to say hi and welcome you."

"Sure," Kay said. "Why don't you come over later? Frank just got a fresh bottle of gas for the grill. Hey, Frank—what are we burning tonight?"

"I don't know. Some kind of dead animal."

"Terrific! Say seven o'clock?"

Alex thought Lucy would decline. She was almost as introverted as he was.

"That sounds great!" said Lucy. She often surprised him.

"Bring swimsuits. The pool service turned on the heater last week."

Alex and Lucy said they would.

"Okay. See you then."

The Hermans said goodbye.

"They seem nice," Alex said on the way back home.

"Kay's a hugger," Lucy said.

"So I noticed."

"Are you okay?"

"Yeah," he said. At least he hadn't recoiled when Kay hugged him. That would have made a bad impression.

"I like them," said Lucy. "Quite an age difference, though."

"Different strokes," said Alex.

"I guess."

Chapter 3

BARBEQUE

When Alex and Lucy came through the gate to the backyard, Kay was setting food on the picnic table: pasta salad, chips, condiments, and other typical picnic food. Frank was at the grill nearby, turning ribs with tongs.

"Right on time," Kay said.

Lucy pulled a bottle out of her beach bag. "I brought some of Mr. Rossetti's homemade wine."

Kay laughed. "Hear that, Frank?"

Frank chuckled.

Kay reached into a cooler and pulled out two similar bottles, one in each hand. "They left a hundred bottles in the basement when they moved. They didn't have anywhere to store it at their new house." Kay opened one of the bottles and filled a wine glass. "I don't know if it's any good, but I'm not picky when alcohol's involved." She took a sip. "A little fancy for my taste, but it'll do." She poured wine into another glass.

"None for me, thanks," said Alex.

"Alex doesn't drink," said Lucy. "He's a little OCD. He's afraid he'll kill brain cells."

"I respect that, although he seems like the kind of guy that could spare a few." Kay filled glasses for Frank and Lucy.

Frank grabbed a platter. "Ribs are done," he announced.

Kay said, "Okay, everybody, let's dig in."

The ribs were juicy and flavorful. Everything was delicious. Alex had never liked pasta salad, but Kay's was tasty.

"How did you two meet?" Lucy asked. The question seemed forward, but Kay didn't seem to mind.

"SugarDaddy dot com," Kay said. Alex and Lucy laughed, thinking it was a joke. "No, for real. I was looking for a handsome guy with money, and I saw a picture of this mature stud with an interesting profile, retired ophthalmologist, and I said, 'That's the guy for me.'"

Lucy and Alex looked at Frank for confirmation. "It's true," he said.

"We had a few dates, hit it off, and a couple of months later, he proposed. His kids and the ex-wife were furious."

"They'll be okay," Frank said. "They'll all get something when I croak."

"It's been a while," Kay said. "They're coming around. How about you two?"

Lucy looked at Alex.

"Go ahead," he said. "You tell it better."

"I went with a friend to Lollapalooza—"

"—July 24th, 1994," said Alex.

"Smashing Pumpkins!" Kay said. "The Beastie Boys! I saw them in Colorado that year!"

"About an hour before the first act, my friend Taylor said, 'Look at that creep.' I look up and this guy's staring at me. He was so intense!"

"Alex?"

"Yep. Guess what he was doing?"

"Undressing you with his eyes?"

Lucy laughed. "He didn't even know I was there. He was inventing the search engine."

"I wasn't inventing it," Alex said. "I was trying to make it better."

"He's being modest," Lucy said. "He laid out the model for Google when we were dating, two years before they launched."

"Anyway," Alex continued, "I was lost in thought, staring into space. When I came back to the real world, I saw the most beautiful woman I'd ever seen."

"Me," Lucy said.

"Taylor gave me the finger, pulled Lucy up, and away they went. I had only noticed her for a second, and she was walking out of my life for good."

"Aw," Kay said. "But obviously, it didn't end there."

"Fast forward to six weeks later, on the first day of fall semester. I had to take an art appreciation class to catch up on my humanities credits. I was waiting for class to start, and this voice behind me said, 'Did you enjoy Lollapalooza?' I turned around, and there she was."

"Like it was Fate," Kay said.

"Whatever happened to good old Taylor?" Alex asked.

Lucy shrugged. "I don't know. You and I started dating, and we lost touch."

"But they all lived happily ever after," Kay said.

They finished eating. Kay wrapped the food and took it inside while the others tidied up.

When Kay returned, she pointed to the treehouse in the corner of the yard.

"I've always wanted a treehouse," she said.

"Mr. Rossetti made it for his son Joey," Lucy said. "Have you been inside?"

"No. You?"

"Our daughter has. She and Joey used to spend a lot of time together."

"Let's go check it out."

Kay stood. Lucy followed.

Frank said, "Be careful, ladies!"

Kay said, "Don't tell me what to do, old man! We're gonna be reckless!"

"Kay's a firecracker," Frank said to Alex.

"So I see."

Lucy said, "You've got an unusual name. Kori tis Thalassis..."

"Yeah."

"What ethnicity is it?"

"Greek. It means 'daughter of the sea.'"

"It's beautiful. Are you Greek?" Lucy asked.

"My adoptive parents were. I grew up on an island south of the mainland called Kythira."

"You don't have an accent."

"I've lived in the US for a while. Lucy—it's from Latin. It means 'light'."

"Yep."

They walked to the base of the tree and looked up.

"I've always wanted to see the inside," said Lucy.

"Well, here's your chance."

Kay climbed the ladder and opened the trap door at the top. She disappeared inside, then poked her head out.

"Come on up!"

Lucy climbed the ladder.

Frank looked at Alex. "What do you do for work?"

"I'm a partner in a small web design company."

"Isn't there a lot of competition in that?"

"Now there is. But we got in early, and we're really good at it."

Kay looked out the window of the treehouse. "Hey, Frank! I can see our house from up here!"

Frank chuckled.

The women climbed down from the treehouse and passed by the pool. They were a beautiful pair.

"We are lucky men," Frank said.

"Yes, we are," Alex agreed.

Kay dipped a toe into the water.

"I don't know," she said. "Tell me what you think."

Lucy slid out of her sandals and tested the water. Kay suddenly pushed her into the pool and laughed.

Frank chuckled again.

Lucy surfaced, thrashing wildly in the water.

"Help!" she cried before submerging again.

Frank was alarmed.

"She's okay," Alex said. "She was on the swim team in high school."

But Kay was horrified. She reached out a hand to Lucy. Lucy thrashed to the side and took Kay's hand, then braced her feet against the side and pulled Kay in.

Frank was relieved. He chuckled again.

Kay surfaced and sputtered. Lucy pushed her hair out of her eyes. "I think the water's fine." She smiled at Kay.

"Bitch!" Kay said. She laughed and splashed Lucy.

Frank shook his head. "Maybe Kay has met her match."

Kay started to take off her shirt. "Hey, Frank, is it too early for skinny-dipping?"

"Careful, dear. We just met these nice people. We don't want to scare them off just yet."

"You're no fun," Kay said.

The women drank wine, frolicked, and swam in their clothes until the sun went down. Then Frank excused himself. "I've got an early tee time tomorrow."

"I should go, too," said Alex. "Thanks for having us over."

"Our pleasure."

"Lucy, I'm heading back to the house."

"Don't go," said Kay. "It's early still."

"I've got things to do."

"Do you mind if I stay?" Lucy asked.

"Not at all. I'm glad you're having fun."

"Thanks for coming," Kay said. "It was nice to meet you."

"You, too."

When he got home, the bedroom was warm and stuffy. He opened the window to let in a breeze.

He could see over the hedges into the Halloways' backyard. A portable stereo was playing music. Kay and Lucy each held a bottle of wine and danced to the Beastie Boys. Alex was a little concerned. Lucy's doctors had cautioned against her mixing her antidepressant with alcohol. But she was having a good time. That was a rare thing. He decided not to worry.

He got into bed and tried to sleep, but the music was loud enough to keep him awake. Eventually, the music stopped. A little while later, Lucy tiptoed into the room.

"Hey, baby," he said.

"You're still awake."

"Yeah. That was fun, wasn't it?"

She crawled into bed. "I had a good time. I really like them." She lay on her side, facing away from him. Alex snuggled against her. "I got tipsy. I haven't done that in a while." Alex kissed her shoulder, then stroked her side. "Could I get a raincheck on that?" she said. "I'm exhausted."

"Sure thing." His head settled on the pillow.

She let him spoon her, and he started to get an erection. He tried to ignore it, thinking it might go away.

"Is that you?" she asked. She laughed.

"What?"

"It feels like some critter trying to crawl up between my butt cheeks."

"Something like an anaconda?"

She snorted. "More like a baby garter snake."

"Yep, that's me. Sorry." He turned over, away from her. "It's got a mind of its own."

"It's a long weekend. We'll find time." She turned, spooned against him, and sighed. Soon she was snoring softly.

Chapter 4

THE CURIO CABINET

Alex and Lucy were having breakfast when the doorbell rang. Alex answered it, and Kay was standing there.

"'Morning, neighbor!" she said. "I was wondering if I could borrow your wife."

"Come on in."

"Hi, Kay!" Lucy said.

"What a beautiful home!" Kay said.

"Come on. I'll give you a tour."

"Maybe later. I got a new credit card yesterday, and I'm dying to break it in. Feel like shopping?"

"Always!"

"You can show me all the good shops."

"That may take a while."

"I have all day. We'll keep going until the card's maxed out." Kay said to Alex, "Frank is having trouble moving some furniture. I was wondering if you could help him out."

"I'll see what I can do," said Alex.

•♥•♥•♥•♥•♥•

Frank sized up the cabinet. It was made of solid oak. He was trying to devise a plan of attack.

"I don't know..." he said. "It's for Kay's what-nots."

"It's beautiful wood," said Alex.

"But it's really heavy."

"Do you have a dolly?" Alex asked, although he wasn't sure what good a dolly would be with a piece of furniture that long and heavy.

"No."

"How about those slider pads like they show on tv?"

"No. Sorry."

"I guess it's brute force, then."

He positioned himself at one end, with Frank on the other. They looked for places to grab the behemoth. There were hand-holds in the back of the cabinet but nothing in the front except one inch of lip, too high to be of much use. It was all they had.

"One, two, three!" They hoisted and shuffled, both men grunting, to the spot where Kay had said she wanted the thing to go. As they lowered it, a pain started in the small of Alex's back and shot down his right leg.

Frank saw Alex grimace. "You okay?"

"Got a bad disk. I should lie down and relax for a while."

"Sorry. I appreciate this. If Kay wants it moved again, we'll hire somebody."

Alex nodded, rubbing his back with one hand.

He had trouble walking home.

When Lucy returned from shopping, Alex was on the bed, laptop on his belly and a pillow under his knees. She was full of energy and smiling.

"Did you have a good time?" he asked.

"I had a great time! That Kay is wild!" She set the bags on the floor and climbed into bed.

She put her lips to his neck and kissed him.

"Want to make love?" she asked.

"Mmm," he said. "I think I do."

She repositioned herself to kiss him on the lips. His back twinged, and he groaned.

"What?" she asked.

He pulled a bag from under his back.

"What's that?" she asked.

"Frozen peas."

"I can see that. I mean, why?"

"To keep the swelling down. The cabinet put up a good fight, but I think we got the better of it."

"Poor baby."

"You really want to have sex?"

"Don't you?"

"Well, yeah," he said. "Why now? It's been months."

She shrugged. "I don't know...I just feel kind of sexy."

"I don't think I can," he said.

"Wow," she said. "You've never turned down sex before. This must be serious."

They discussed the options—off to the ER for immediate treatment or the wait-and-see approach. Alex thought with enough frozen peas and ibuprofen, he'd make a full recovery, but if his back wasn't better by Tuesday morning, he'd make an appointment.

Alex babied his back all day Monday, but the pain worsened. He stayed in bed, tracking website traffic, catching up on the news, and watching TED talks, all from his bed on the laptop. He only got up to use the toilet, and every time it was a painful ordeal.

Hannah got back from her training just before dinner. She tapped on the door jamb.

He looked up from the laptop. "Hey, kiddo. How was the training?"

"Too cold to swim. Got real intimate with a CPR dummy." She looked at him with empathy. "The back again?"

"Yeah. It might be time for surgery."

She nodded with sympathy. "Mom's making a casserole. I'll bring you some when it's ready."

"Thanks."

"Let me know if you need anything. Love you, Dad."

"Love you, too."

Chapter 5

VENUS IN TWILIGHT

Alex was in bed, watching a TED talk on the laptop, earbuds in his ears. Lucy entered the bedroom and stripped off her clothes. She put on an oversized t-shirt and climbed into bed. She kissed him on the head and said, "Goodnight."

She started a crossword puzzle. A few minutes later, her eyes were closed, and the book rested on her chest.

Alex removed his earbuds and stowed his laptop on the shelf of his nightstand. He went to the bathroom one more time. He took two more ibuprofen.

He turned out the light on Lucy's side of the bed. She began snoring as he settled back in. He gave it a fair amount of time, but between Lucy's snoring and the pain, falling asleep was a losing battle. He got to his feet slowly, grabbed his pillow, and hobbled down the hall to the spare bedroom.

The room was hot and stuffy. He put the pillow on the bed and opened the window.

The sun had just set. There was a soft orange glow between the leaves and branches of the trees. The street lights were turning on one by one.

He looked down on the Holloways' backyard. Kay sat at the pool in a bikini, legs dangling in the water, drinking wine straight from the bottle. He wondered what it would be like to be with Kay. Old Frank was indeed a lucky man.

When he first met Kay, she had struck him as a hyperactive tomboy. Now she embodied the divine feminine. Alex tried to look away, but her body called to him, *Worship me...*

Kay set the wine down and stood. A blue aura surrounded her, a trick of the moonlight and tiki torches, Alex thought.

Kay slowly pulled the bikini top up off her torso, over her head, and off her arms. She dropped it onto the patio.

Alex was shocked.

She hooked her thumbs into the waist of her bikini bottoms, slid them down to the deck, and stepped out of them.

Alex lost his balance and knocked over the table lamp beside the window. It crashed on its side on the top of the nightstand. He righted the lamp and looked out the window again to make sure Kay hadn't heard, wouldn't know he'd been spying on her.

But she was looking directly at the house, at him. She knew he was there. She raised a hand to her mouth and blew him a kiss. She dove into the pool.

He was uneasy. He went to the bed and lay down.

He thought she had been joking about skinny dipping the other night because—who really did that? She did, evidently.

He *had* been spying on her. He *was* being creepy. And he was turned on in a very inappropriate way. But...

She had blown him a kiss.

He didn't know what to make of that.

Chapter 6

PRIMARY CARE

"Yes," the doctor said. "That pesky disk between L4 and L5."

The doctor was an older, jolly man with an Eastern European accent. He held an electronic tablet and sent an image of Alex's spine to a large monitor. With a stylus, he drew a circle around a space between two vertebrae. It didn't look right.

"What do we do?" Alex asked.

"Surgery is the best option now. At this point, it will never heal on its own."

"I was afraid of that."

The doctor patted him gently on the shoulder. "It's okay. Two hours in the care of a surgeon, during which you'll be unconscious, and when you wake up, you'll be as good as new. Well, six to eight weeks of gradual recovery. Sound good?"

Alex nodded.

"They'll give you a referral when you check out. Call that number to schedule the surgery. In the meantime, do you need something for the pain?"

"Yes, please."

The doctor pulled out a prescription pad. "Are opioids okay? I only pull out the big guns when I have to, but I think, in your case, they are called for."

"Yeah. It hurts like crazy."

The doctor filled out the form and handed it to Alex. "How's everything other than the back?"

Alex sighed. "I feel like an old man," he said.

The doctor chuckled. "Wait until you're my age."

Alex wasn't amused.

The doctor's expression sobered. He gave Alex a closer look. "Something else is going on? Do you think you might be experiencing depression?"

"That's a strong word," Alex said. "Intense mid-life crisis, maybe?"

"Please elaborate."

"It's hard to get excited about anything. And it seems like it's just going to get worse from here on. Your back goes out, you go bald, your prostate causes problems, and your joints give out. Heart disease, high blood pressure, cancer. Et cetera, et cetera."

"This sounds like mild depression to me," said the doctor. "Please stop talking before you get *me* depressed." He looked at Alex with sympathy. "As we age, some things get better, and some get worse. What do you do for fun?"

"I enjoy my work."

"Yes, but you need more. A hobby, exercise. Are you having good sex?"

"That's part of the problem."

"Is all of the equipment working?"

"Yeah. What I need is a willing partner. My wife has put me in the friend zone. She got frisky the other day, right after I wrecked my back, ironically. The first time in months."

The doctor chuckled.

"Her timing is impeccable!" he said. "If I remember correctly, Mrs. Herman takes an antidepressant? One of the older ones?"

"Yes."

"They can reduce the libido. Has she tried one of the newer ones?"

Alex nodded.

"They weren't as effective."

"I can give you a referral for a sex therapist."

"I don't think so ."

"So you're gonna tough it out, Mr. Macho?"

"Maybe we've been together so long that I've literally bored the fuck out of her. What do you do for that?"

The doctor smiled compassionately.

"Maybe. It happens." He sighed. "We don't have to solve all of your problems today. Let's take care of the back. Then we will live one day at a time and find a solution. We'll live a good life, and many years from now, God willing, die a good death. Am I right?"

The doctor's words were oddly comforting.

When Alex pulled into his driveway, Kay was trimming the hedges between the two houses. She waved as he struggled out of the car.

"Hey, neighbor!" she said.

"Kay," he said as he hobbled closer.

"How's the back? Lucy told me." Kay was wearing a bikini top and very short cut-off jeans.

"They're recommending surgery."

"I'm sorry." She sighed. "I feel responsible. It wouldn't have happened if I had told the movers where I wanted that monstrosity. I couldn't make up my mind."

"It's not your fault. I've had a bad back for years."

"Still..." she said. "I hear you're sleeping in the spare room."

"Yeah."

"How's the view from up there?" She smiled. She was flirting.

He wanted to flirt back without being creepy. He chose his words carefully.

"I saw a full moon last night. It was breathtaking."

She picked up on the double meaning and smiled. "See you later, neighbor."

"See you later."

She continued trimming her hedges.

Lucy was in the kitchen when he got inside.

"What did the doctor say?" she asked.

"They want to operate."

"Good. Then we'll get it taken care of."

He tore open the bag that had his bottle of Percocet. He twisted the cap off, shook out a pill, put it in his mouth, and swallowed it dry. He handed Lucy a note.

"This is the number for the surgeon's office. Could you make the call for me? First available."

"Sure."

He sat slowly at the breakfast nook.

"Kay and I hung out by the pool for a while today. I really like her."

"She's quite a character."

"You don't know the half of it! I don't know whether she's loco or I've just had a sheltered life."

"Probably a little of both. I heard her swimming last night." He didn't mention that he *saw* her, *all* of her. It was better if he didn't share the details.

"If I had a pool, I'd be swimming all the time."

"I'm going to lie down for a while."

"I'm making chicken alfredo and broccoli."

"Sounds good."

"Be careful going up the stairs."

"I will."

He went to the spare room, put one pillow under his knees, one under his head, and the laptop on his belly, and tried to work. But soon, the painkiller had him in its spell.

He drifted off to sleep and dreamed of the beautiful lady next door.

Chapter 7
THE DREAM

It was too vivid to be a dream, but too fantastic to be anything but. He was lucid, and all his senses were engaged.

He was lying on a beach. Waves crashed in front of him. He slowly stood and looked around. A full moon was rising to his left. The sun had just set on his right. The planet Venus shone brightly overhead. He was dressed only in a coarsely woven loin cloth.

"Come, my love!" said a voice behind him. "Come join the celebration!"

He turned to see Kay standing at the top of a grassy dune. She spoke a language he had never heard before, but he understood her. She was alluring. She wore only a bronze chain around her waist and a crown of wildflowers. She held out her hand to him. "Come. They are waiting."

"Who?" he asked.

"My people," she said. "You will be my priest tonight."

He climbed the dune and took her hand. He looked down the slope on the far side. A crowd of celebrants danced in a circle around a bonfire, while others played wooden flutes and drums. It looked like some kind of Pagan fertility ritual.

Where were they?

Maybe more importantly, *when* were they? A wall of ice reached to the sky in the distance to the North.

Kay led him down the slope. As they approached, the celebrants bowed to them and smiled. They chanted, "Kori! Kori! Kori tis Thalassis!"

Kay held Alex's hand up high, and the celebrants cheered.

She led him to a tent. Inside was a small fire and a deep pile of furs. She gestured to this bed. She wanted him to lie on it, so he did.

He knew what was about to happen, and he wondered if he should feel guilty.

No, this is just a dream.

She got on top of him and kissed him. The dream was so vivid he could smell her, a sweet musk with notes of the sea, mixed with the scent of the fire. She was in control here. He was just a willing victim. No—an eager partner. She bowed her head and kissed him. He felt her lips, warm, wet, and supple. He tasted them and realized how hungry he'd been. His inhibitions fell away. They kissed and caressed as the people outside chanted and danced.

She locked eyes with him, reached down, and moved his loin cloth out of her way. She guided him inside her. Their bodies fit together perfectly. She rocked her pelvis slowly, and he began to thrust, following her rhythm.

"*Feel the power of this union, my love?*" Kay said without speaking.

Yes...

It was a few minutes or an eternity. Time had no meaning. It was magic. The pleasure was more intense than his mind could grasp. As he approached climax, Kay said, "And the high gods created the cosmos in just this way!"

There was a blinding flash of light.

He woke.

Well, that was interesting, he thought.

He'd had plenty of crazy dreams in his life, many of them erotic, but that had been a doozie.

He lay there for a while and savored the memory. The dream tryst might have been better than the real thing.

He looked at his phone. He had slept through the night. The alarm was set to go off in another ten minutes.

He rose and got ready for work.

Chapter 8

SOLO OF TWO

Alex hobbled into the conference room at Tucker-Herman and sat carefully in the chair to Madison's left.

She noticed he was walking strangely and gave him a quizzical look. "We missed you yesterday," she said. "What happened? Brad wouldn't say."

"I hurt my back," Alex said. "Again. Bad disk."

"Ouch." She winced. "How bad is it?"

"I need surgery."

"Sorry to hear that."

Lilith said to the group, "I had a dream last night that I went to Cancun. How do I get a passport?"

"Here," said Bob. "Why don't I google that for you?"

Garth snickered.

"Jerk," she replied.

Garth made an eerie whistle, like the soundtrack of a monster movie. "I dreamed that I worked with intelligent people. And yet, here we are."

Brad entered the room and sat at the head of the conference table. "How was everyone's weekend?" he asked.

The staff replied in the affirmative.

"Just awesome," said Alex.

Brad looked at him. "Welcome back. Are you okay?"

"I will be, eventually."

"While you have the floor, is there anything you'd like to say to Bob?"

Alex looked across the table to Bob, who looked uncomfortable with the attention. "No, I'm good," Alex said.

Brad sighed, and continued in a voice louder than usual. "What Alex wants to say, Bob, is that he'd like his metadata loaded to the new pages for the Faygo website."

"I'm working on it."

"It was supposed to be done at launch on Friday."

"I don't understand why it's so important."

Garth said, "Don't..."

Bob continued. "Google doesn't look at keywords anymore."

Everyone groaned in unison.

"You don't know that," said Garth.

"It's common knowledge. Headers, incoming links, hypertext, and copy carry the weight."

Lilith chimed in. "The algorithms are secret."

"My information comes from official statements from Google." Bob was getting loud and defensive.

Brad rapped his knuckles loudly on the desk. "Children, children!"

When it was quiet again, Alex spoke. "Google never said that keywords were completely out of the formula, so we don't know their weight in the algorithm. And what about people who use other search engines? Like Bing or Baidu?"

"Losers!" Bob said. He knew it was a mistake before it came out of his mouth.

"Users in China are losers?" asked Lilith. "I'm only asking because some of our clients do a lot of business in China where—guess what?— they don't have Google."

"You go, Lilith," said Garth.

"Listen," Brad said. "I don't want our clients to lose a single customer because someone here is taking shortcuts. Feel free to question anything, and we'll have a discussion. But one thing I will not allow is telling us you'll do something, then not doing it. Understood?"

Bob's face was red. "Yes, sir."

Brad leaned forward. "Now we discuss punishment."

Bob squirmed.

"Any Ideas?" Brad asked.

"Exile," said Garth.

Brad looked around the room. No one objected. "Exile it is. Length of sentence?"

"One week," said Lilith.

"I don't know. That seems light."

"You should consider that you chewed Bob out in the conference room instead of privately."

"Very well. My apologies, Bob. I could have handled it better. I now proclaim that you are banned from the pit for one week." Brad rapped his knuckles on the desk again.

Bob breathed a sigh of relief.

"Very good," Brad said. "Everyone's dismissed except for the sales department."

They all got to their feet except Madison, because she *was* the sales department. Alex started to rise, but Madison touched him on the arm and said, "Hang on a second."

The staff filtered out until it was just Brad, Alex, and Madison.

"Weren't you a little hard on Bob?" asked Alex.

"We've got a great team here, but sometimes you have to show them who the alphas are. He won't be taking shortcuts again, and he'll be a better employee because of it." He looked at Madison. "Are you ready for your first solo?"

"I'm ready, but I'd like Alex to come along. The prospects had technical questions that I couldn't answer. And they wanted to meet the guy that invented the internet." She laughed.

"I didn't invent the internet," said Alex.

"Well, they seem to think you did. And it's not my job to convince them otherwise. It might help me seal the deal."

"My back is killing me."

"It's what the prospect wants. You want my first solo to be a success, don't you?" She batted her eyes at him comically.

"Of course. But how is it a solo if I go along?"

"I'll do the presentation. You won't have to say anything unless someone asks something technical."

"We could make millions off these people," said Brad. "But we have to hook them first."

Brad and Alex locked eyes in a battle of wills. Alex blinked first. "Okay," said Alex. "Okay."

"Great," Brad said. "Madison, go prepare. I need to speak with Alex."

"Yes, boss."

After she was out of the room, Brad said, "The Landy awards—September 18th. I can't make it this year. I need you to go for me."

"Why does anyone have to go?"

"Someone needs to represent Tucker-Herman."

"Anyone could go. Garth, Lilith."

"I'd prefer a grown-up."

"I don't know."

"You won't have to network. Take Lucy. Make it a long weekend. Sightseeing, maybe some romance."

Alex pondered.

"Seattle?" He asked.

"Yep."

"Lucy's never been."

"Great. You can leave early, have a good time, and come back late."

"It does sound like fun."

"Good. Decide how much time you want to spend there, and I'll make the reservations."

Madison was waiting for Alex when he got back to his office. She had a messenger bag for her laptop and presentation materials.

"I'm all set," she said. "But you could take your clothes up another notch."

"You think?" He opened the small closet in the corner of the room. "Dress shirt?"

"And blazer," she said.

"Tie?"

"No. You want to project 'eccentric genius,' not 'corporate ass-kisser.'"

"Okay."

"How's your back?"

"I'll be fine once I get another one of those pills in me." He looked at his watch. "We should get going."

"Right."

"Will you excuse me while I change clothes?"

"Oh. Of course."

He met her in the lobby after he had changed.

"Looking good, boss!" she said.

"Thanks." He held the door open for her. "I'm still not comfortable. I'm not exactly a people person."

"So I've noticed. You'll be fine," she said. "This way. My car."

"Good," he said. "Do you know where we're going?"

"The phone does." She held her phone to her mouth. "Find directions to two thousand Brush Street, Detroit, Michigan." She hit the unlock button on her key fob.

As they left the parking lot, Alex looked at her in profile. She was pretty, but not in a glamorous way—that would have made Alex uncomfortable. And she looked familiar for some reason.

She caught him looking at her.

"I'm trying to figure out who you remind me of," he said.

She smiled.

After they got onto the freeway, Alex reached into the inner pocket of his blazer for his bottle of Percocets. He opened it and fished one out.

"Careful with those," said Madison. "That's why I'm divorced."

"That's funny. You don't look like a substance abuser."

She laughed.

"Lars. The rock star wannabe." She handed him a water bottle to wash the pill down. He looked at the bottle and hesitated. "No cooties, I swear," she said. "His band came to Detroit to get some street cred."

"That's a thing?"

"I don't know. It didn't help. Before I knew it, he was spending more money on pills than we could afford with our combined incomes. Then he graduated to heroin because it was cheaper."

"You've been through a lot."

"Lesson learned. I'm done with man-boys. I'm going to give you some advice: please be careful with those pills. Don't get hooked."

"Thanks. I won't." He looked sincere. "My dream is to become an alcoholic."

She laughed.

"Do you have any of the ex's music?"

"Why?"

"I used to be a metalhead."

"Sure. On my phone." He picked up her phone and looked at the display. "Hit the music icon. It's under 'Grand Maul, M-A-U-L.'"

"Clever name."

"Sadly, the name is the best thing about them."

He hit the play button on the screen. Loud music filled the car.

"They're not horrible," he said.

Madison shrugged.

The pain meds were making him tired. He turned off the music.

"I'm going to take a little nap," he said.

"Go ahead. You have time."

The sound of wheels on pavement lulled him to sleep.

He felt the car come to a stop.

"Wakey wakey," Madison said. "We're here."

He opened his eyes. They were in a parking structure. She handed him a cup of coffee.

"I went through the drive-through at Tim Horton's," she said.

He took a sip. "Thanks," he said. "How far away are we?"

"They're right around the corner. We have twenty minutes."

"Good. I need time to wake up."

Madison set the timer on her phone, closed her eyes, and meditated while Alex drank his coffee.

When the timer went off, Madison looked at him and said, "Okay, let's do this."

In the office building lobby, Madison asked, "How's your back?"

"Good, for now." He pressed the button for the elevator.

"Remember, this is *my* sales call. Everyone knows who you are, but I'll introduce you anyway. Smile, shake hands, and be social. You won't have to say anything unless someone asks a technical question."

The elevator doors opened, and they entered.

"Do you have everything you need?" He asked.

"Oh, please."

"Sorry. It's the OCD."

"I was nineteen the last time I screwed up a presentation."

"I'm not used to someone so young being so confident."

She smiled. "How young do you think I am?"

"Will this get me into trouble?"

"Not at all."

"I'd say... twenty-five." She just smiled. "Am I right?" She didn't reply. "Am I close?"

The door opened, and they made their way to the prospect's conference room.

Alex was impressed with the way Madison handled herself during her sales pitch. She compared the costs of advertising on the web versus print and broadcast media. She made a case for Tucker-Herman being their best choice for web design and site maintenance. The executives were hooked by the end of her presentation.

"Are there any questions?" she asked at the end.

A young man spoke. He looked like he had just graduated from business school. "Do you do A/B testing?"

"Hmm," Madison said. "That's not my area of expertise. I'll let Alex answer that one."

All eyes turned to Alex.

"We do A through Z testing," Alex said. "We're meticulous."

"Do you take down your low-traffic pages?" the young man asked.

"No," Alex said.

"Why not? Doesn't that dilute the ranking of the higher traffic pages?" The young man was trying to show how clever he was.

"Yes, if you do it wrong. If you do it right, the low traffic pages create a synergy that boosts the rankings of the high traffic pages."

"How?" the young man asked.

"Sign a contract, and I'll tell you. I was doing this before they coined the term 'search engine optimization.' I'm not giving away all that experience for free."

Was he being overly assertive? Whatever. He was telling the truth.

It seemed to work. The head of the advertising firm nodded.

"Fair enough," the head man said. "We need to talk it over, but I like what we've heard. I'll call Brad tomorrow with our decision."

Madison smiled and packed her materials. Alex shook hands on his way out.

They were nonchalant as they made their way to the elevator. Alex pressed the down button.

"That went well," said Alex.

"Yes, it did."

"You really know what you're doing."

"Why, thank you. We make a pretty good team."

The door opened, and Alex gestured. "After you."

They entered the elevator, and the doors closed. He raised his hand to give her a high five, but she hugged him instead. He tensed. She quickly let him go.

"I'm sorry," she said. "That was unprofessional."

"It's okay."

"I got carried away. My first pitch, and they're going to sign on. Is it your back?"

"No. You... just... caught me off-guard."

Madison was quiet on the way back to the car, no longer her bubbly self.

When they returned to the freeway, Alex asked, "What's the matter?"

"Nothing. Why?"

"You were happy, and now you're sad."

"I'm a hugger."

"I figured that out."

"I'm sorry if I crossed a line."

"It's not you. It's me. I like hugs. I just need a little warning."

"Okay."

"I have issues," he said. "I'm on the autism spectrum."

She was surprised. "You could have fooled me."

"Forty years of practice, trying to pass for normal."

"Thanks for sharing that with me," she said.

They were quiet on the way back to the office.

A few weeks later, they saw each other in the hall. She looked sad. Her eyes were red and puffy.

"Are you okay?" he asked.

"No," she replied. "Can I have a hug?"

"Of course."

She put her arms around him and started to cry.

"Oh," he said. "Please don't." He put his arms around her, too. He was uncomfortable at first. He hadn't been touched in a while. Then he relaxed and leaned into it. Her body was cushy. Her hair smelled nice.

It seemed like it went on forever. Finally, she let him go, looked him in the eyes, and said, "Thank you."

"Better?" he asked.

She nodded and smiled. The clouds had passed.

She never told him what had made her cry, and he never asked. If she had needed to talk, she would have.

It was disturbing. He hoped he'd never have to see a woman cry, ever again.

But he frequently remembered that hug. That one was special.

Chapter 9

THE OPERATION

Alex dreaded the surgery. He tossed and turned the night before. He was afraid something would go wrong, but he also looked forward to being pain-free someday.

When it was time, Lucy tiptoed into the spare room and stroked his arm. "Six o'clock, sweetie. Time to go." He slowly got to his feet, put on sweatpants and a T-shirt, and carefully descended the stairs.

Lucy filled a travel mug with coffee. "Do you want some?" she asked.

"Can't. No food, no fluids."

"Oh, that's right."

She had an overnight bag packed and waiting by the door. He slowly bent to pick it up, out of habit. The pain and pain meds made him loopy.

"I've got that," she said and opened the door for him.

He headed for the driver's side of the car.

"No, silly," she said. "I'm driving."

"Oh, of course."

"Thanks for taking care of me," he said on the way to the hospital.

She smiled. "My pleasure. You're really not much work."

She parked the car at the patient drop-off and helped him into a wheelchair. She wheeled him to the reception desk, and he filled out his paperwork while she parked the car.

When Lucy returned, a nurse wheeled him to his room. Another helped him into his bed and checked his vitals. An anesthetist came and inserted a drip into his arm.

"How's your pain level, Mr. Herman?" she asked. "On a scale from one to ten."

"Twelve," he said.

"It's going to be a few more hours, but we'll try to make you comfortable." She ran a line from a machine into a port on his IV tube. She handed him a control pendant and pointed. "When you need some relief, just press this button."

Alex pressed the button right away, and the machine beeped. The pain diminished just a little. He waited a while, then hit the button again. The machine beeped again.

Lucy kissed him on the forehead. "I'll see you when you wake up. Love you, baby."

He looked at her, but his eyes wouldn't focus. He tried to speak, but no sound came out. The pain persisted. He hit the button again, three times. Finally, the pain diminished to the point where it was bearable.

Well, thank God for anesthesia, he said to himself. *It was a better invention than the light bulb.*

Consciousness slipped away. Doctors and nurses came and went. A young man on the tv sold fantastic machines that could give you a rock-hard body with six-pack abs that would make you envied by other men and desired by women. It was all surreal.

The surgery was successful. They discharged him after twenty-four hours. He worked from home and healed.

Chapter 10

PICNIC

Alex set the cooler on the tile inside the front door. He wore sunglasses, a tacky Hawaiian shirt, sandals, and khaki shorts over his swim trunks.

"Are you sure you don't want to come?" he called to Lucy, who was reading a book in the living room.

"I'm not going out in this heat for one of Brad's social events. Kay and I are going to hang out by the pool."

"It'll be just as hot there."

"But arm's length from clean water and air conditioning."

"Suit yourself. Come on by if you change your mind."

"Will do. Have a good time."

"You, too."

"Tell Brad I said hi. Don't forget to put on sunscreen!" she said as he closed the door.

It was the Fourth of July weekend, and the park was crowded.

Brad had a picnic structure reserved between the river and the canoe livery, and Alex found him there, sitting at the picnic table with a beer in his hand.

Alex placed the cooler on the concrete slab. "Hey, bro."

"Hey. How's the back?"

"Feels great. I'm hoping for a limbo competition later."

Brad laughed. "Don't get carried away."

Bob and Garth were nearby playing frisbee. Lilith was on a blanket in the shade of a willow tree.

He heard Madison's voice. "Hey, guys!" He turned. She wore a big floppy hat and a blue one-piece bathing suit. "What's on the agenda?"

"There's no agenda, child. Just relaxation and social intercourse."

Madison snickered. "He said 'intercourse.'"

"I heard," Alex said.

"Well, my top priority is to get some sun on this pasty skin," Madison said. She took her blanket to an empty spot on the grass, close enough to Lilith to talk to her but with enough distance to make it an option. "Hey, girlfriend!"

Alex took two iced teas out of the cooler and followed her. He helped her spread the blanket and handed her an iced tea after she sat. He sat next to her.

"What's with Brad?" she asked.

"What do you mean?"

"He called me 'child.'"

"He's irritated," Alex said.

"Did I do something?"

"Oh, no. He doesn't approve."

"Of what?"

"You and I being friends."

"Are you kidding me?"

"He's afraid we'll get...you know...involved."

She frowned. "That's ridiculous."

"I know. I'm married, and old enough to be your father."

"Just how old are you, anyway?"

"Forty-three."

"It's possible, I suppose...if you knocked up my mother when you were ten. Were you ever in Milwaukee around that time ?"

"No." Alex laughed and took a drink. "He's a little paranoid. There was a lawsuit a few years ago."

"Involving you?"

Alex laughed. "Involving him."

"Well, that figures."

Lilith chuckled.

"Yeah," she said. "Major mistake with *that* woman."

"Maybe we should dial it back a little," Alex said.

"I was thinking just the opposite. Screw him. He's a good boss, but he doesn't get to control me." She handed Alex a bottle of tanning lotion. "Here, put some of this on my back."

"Are you sure?"

She smiled and batted her eyes.

"Pretty please?"

"Whatever you say."

Madison lay on her belly. Alex took the cap off the lotion and looked at Brad. Brad glared. Alex smiled as he applied the white cream to Madison's back.

"Pretend that you're enjoying it," Madison said.

"That won't be hard," he said. "I *am* enjoying it."

She gave him a coy smile.

Lilith laughed.

After her back and legs were slathered, he lay next to her. They basked silently for a while. The timer on her phone went off.

"That side's done," she said, and they turned over.

His hand accidentally touched hers, and he pulled back. He was surprised when her pinkie wrapped itself around his. It was a little weird, but nice. They stayed that way, pinkies intertwined, until the timer went off again.

"What now?" she asked, sitting up.

"Are you hungry?"

"Not yet."

"How about renting a kayak?"

"How about a pedal boat? That way, we can talk."

They went to the livery and paid for a boat. They were trying on life preservers when Hannah walked up. She stood back and watched them.

"I don't know why we have to wear these," Madison said. "It's not deep enough to drown."

"And yet someone drowns every year," he said.

"Dad?" Hannah said.

"Hey, kiddo. This is my friend Madison. Madison, my daughter Hannah. She works here."

Hannah sized up Madison.

"You two work together?" Hannah asked, frowning.

"Yeah."

"Canoes or kayaks?"

"Pedal boat, please." He showed his receipt to Hannah, who ignored it.

She led them down the dock to a pedal boat and knelt to steady it as they boarded. Madison got the feel of the steering while Hannah untied the line. Alex started pedaling.

"Off we go!" Madison said. "Nice to meet you, Hannah!"

Hannah gave a half-hearted wave from the dock.

Madison waited until they got out of earshot and said, "I don't think she likes me."

Alex had noticed how frosty the interaction was. It wasn't like Hannah.

"It's not you. Maybe she's having a bad day."

They pedaled in silence for a while.

"What beautiful weather!" Madison said at last.

"Yeah, this is nice. I haven't been outdoors in a while."

"You work too much. You have to live a little."

"My work is my life."

"You poor man!" she said. "Well, we'll fix that. I'm going to make you my project."

Alex groaned.

"Don't worry," she said. "It'll be fun."

"Oh, boy."

The Huron River widened, becoming a lake with a slow, gentle current.

She steered them to the middle and stopped pedaling. He stopped pedaling, too. They drifted slowly and took in the view. A thousand people lay out in the sun, played frisbee, or walked their dogs. Madison smiled. Alex was becoming attached to that smile.

"This is the day The Lord has made," she said. "We will rejoice and be glad in it."

"Amen," Alex said, guessing it was the appropriate response.

"I feel really close to God right now," she said. "Are you religious?"

"Not especially. I'm an open-minded skeptic. I know there's something really big going on, but our minds don't have the capacity to understand it. We're like ants on the surface of The Mona Lisa. One ant sees part of the smile, one aunt sees part of an eye. We're not capable of seeing the whole picture."

"And that's why they call it The Great Mystery."

"How about you?"

"We went to church a lot when I was a kid," she said.

"Let me guess. Roman Catholic, parochial school?"

She was surprised. "How'd you know?"

"There's something about you that's, um, angelic? And your posture. Catholic girls all have good posture."

She laughed. "Yeah, it only takes a couple of whacks from a ruler, and you have good posture for life. Shoulders back, tits out. Those poor nuns didn't have a clue what they were doing."

They meandered around the lake, dodging ducks, swans, and lily pads, and talked until it was time to return the boat. They met their coworkers under the shelter for hot dogs and chips.

Whatever problem Brad had had with them, he was over it. He acted as though there was nothing wrong in the world.

And on this gorgeous day, there really wasn't.

Chapter 11

HAPPY ANNIVERARY!

At lunch on July 24th, Madison and Alex sat together, as they had done since Madison's first day at Tucker-Herman.

"We're going to The Grotto for drinks tonight," Madison said. "Wanna come along? Brad's buying."

"Just the first round," Brad said. "I don't want anyone to get the wrong idea."

"Who's going?" Alex asked.

"Everyone, I think," Madison said.

Alex looked at his watch to verify the date again. "I can't," he said. "It's my anniversary."

"You must be confused," Brad said. "You got married in April. I remember because I was your best man."

"Not my wedding. Pine Knob. Lollapalooza."

"You're hopeless," Brad said.

"I'm stepping up my game." He wasn't a romantic by nature. He was trying to do better.

"What?" Madison asked.

"The first time he ever saw his wife."

"That is so...mushy," said Bob.

Lilith looked up from her salad. "That attitude is why you can't keep a girlfriend."

"Anyway," Alex continued, "I've made dinner reservations at Weber's. Can I leave early? I'm all caught up on my work. I need to buy flowers before I get home."

"You're a partner. You can do what you want."

"Thanks," Alex said and finished his sandwich. "Have a good weekend," he said to Madison. "I'll see you Monday."

He returned to his office and packed his laptop.

The lady at the flower shop suggested asters. She put together an arrangement for him. Alex was sure Lucy would be pleased.

He parked the car, quietly unlocked the front door, took his shoes off in the entryway, and carried the bouquet into the kitchen. Lucy wasn't there.

He heard a voice upstairs. He crept up the steps. He couldn't wait to see the look on her face. As he got to the bedroom doorway, he realized it was *two* voices. He peeked around the edge of the door—

—and he was sitting behind his desk at Tucker-Herman, staring out the window.

He was bewildered. He looked at his hands. The walls. The computer monitor.

Evidently, he had dissociated.

There was a knock on the door. He was too shaken to answer. The door opened anyway.

"I thought you were gone for the day," said Madison.

"I thought so, too."

"Are you ok?"

"I don't know."

She looked concerned.

"Should I call an ambulance?"

"No, no," he said. "I'm fine. Really." He was anything but fine, but he didn't want her to worry.

There was an awkward pause.

"Are you coming to the bar tonight?" she asked.

"I don't know what I'm going to do."

She noticed the bouquet on his desk. "Nice flowers. Let me put them in some water for you." She picked them up.

"Oh, the flowers," he said. "Thanks."

Madison left.

The asters...

He'd dissociated once before. Only once, but it had been horrible. He felt a hard knot in his stomach.

Suddenly he was worried about Lucy. He picked up the landline phone on his desk and dialed her cell phone.

It was answered on the third ring.

"Hello," Lucy said.

She was okay. Alex was relieved. He tried to speak but couldn't. He hung up the phone.

What the hell happened?

At the mention of the flowers, the images started coming back to him, out of sequence, in bits and bytes. He tried to stitch them back together so they would make sense.

The break room: he tells everyone goodbye. He says to Madison, "I'll see you Monday."

The flower shop: the lady behind the counter says, "Your anniversary! Congratulations! How many years has it been?"

"Twenty," he says.

"Twenty years. That would be asters," she says. "I'll put something together for you." She disappears into the back and returns a minute later with a bouquet.

"Very nice," he says. He hands her his debit card.

He pulls into the driveway. He enters the front door and removes his shoes. He hears Lucy's voice upstairs. He tiptoes up the steps.

Close to the bedroom door: Lucy says, "I smell flowers.

Kay says, "I smell vanilla."

"That's my body wash."

"Mmmmm."

He peeks around the doorway:

Lucy and Kay...

In bed...

Naked...

Oh, he said to himself.

Oh!

Happy anniversary!

Chapter 12

ODD DUCK

Alex had always been different. His parents knew it before he started kindergarten.

His mother found, to her surprise, that he could read before he was three. She didn't know how it happened. She hadn't put any effort into teaching him aside from introducing him to the alphabet and reading to him every day. But one day, while cleaning the living room, she heard him reading a Dr. Seuss book, One Fish, Two Fish. It caught her off guard, but she told herself they had read it so many times that surely he had memorized it. She took a break from the housecleaning and sat beside him on the floor as he finished.

"Very good, Alex!" she said. "Could you read another one to me?"

"Yes. Pick one, and I'll read it to you."

She picked Goodnight Moon from the bookshelf and handed it to him. He read it aloud flawlessly. There was zero chance that he could have memorized both books. It was akin to a miracle.

He was curious about things most kids, even most adults, never thought about.

One summer day, they found a spider web in the backyard, but there was no sign of a spider.

"Let's see if we can coax her out," his mother said. She picked up a twig and gently touched the bottom edge of the web. Sure enough, the spider came out to see if it had caught any dinner.

"So that's a spider," he said. "What does a cob look like?"

"What do you mean? Like a corn cob?"

"Like a cobweb. Like at grandma's house." He reasoned that if a spider makes a spider web, a cob must make a cobweb.

His mother was amused at the three-year-old's logic. It made perfect sense, but she had to disappoint him. "Nothing makes a cobweb. They just happen." As soon as she said it, though, she began to wonder. What natural process could possibly make a cobweb?

Alex's mother was intelligent and knew a lot, but now they were both skeptical. They went to the set of encyclopedias to do research. They discovered that cobwebs didn't just happen and were, in fact, built by different species of spiders so small and shy that no one ever saw them. And evidently, they were sloppy builders because cobwebs never had the beautiful geometry of a conventional spider web.

Alex could relate to these spiders. He, too, was small, shy, and could be very sloppy.

He had a hard time when he started kindergarten. He missed his mom, his home, his toys, and his books. Kindergarten boys were loud, competitive, and frequently mean. On a bad day, they'd rough him up and call him a sissy. He was more comfortable around girls. They were more civilized.

At the first parent-teacher conference, his teacher expressed concern that Alex wasn't socializing normally.

"Why should he?" his mother asked. "He isn't normal." She said it with a hint of contempt for the teacher. "Give him books, and he'll be fine." So, many times while the other children were playing with blocks, big crayons, and jigsaw puzzles, Alex was in the school library reading the World Book Encyclopedia.

He decided to read the whole thing from A to Z.

Kindergarten set the pattern for Alex's public education.

Chapter 13

CONTROL

Alex was a sensitive kid. He was proud of his intellect but was easily embarrassed when he made a mistake. He felt joy at times and expressed it. He felt sadness at other times and expressed that, too. He cried occasionally, although he learned in kindergarten that if he had to cry, he'd better hold off until after school. Otherwise, he'd be ridiculed for weeks.

The emotional control started in second grade.

The school day usually started with show and tell. Students would stand at their desks one at a time and inform the class about anything interesting they experienced in their lives.

Barbara Aiken had found a pretty rock. She held it up.

Metamorphic, Alex thought. *Agate, probably.*

Sarah Barnette sat to Alex's left. He adored her. She was always very nice to him. Today she had pigtails and was dressed in her Brownie uniform.

She looked upset. She raised her hand.

"Yes, Sarah?"

Sarah stood. "My mom and dad let me watch the news last night." Her eyes filled with tears. "There was a plane crash. Seventy people died."

The teacher said, "I saw that, too. It's really sad, isn't it?"

Sarah sat. The room got very quiet as the students contemplated death, some of them for the first time. The only sound was Sarah Barnette crying her eyes out.

Alex tried to comfort her. He whispered. "You can't let that sadness live in your mind. You'll go crazy."

Sarah nodded and wiped her eyes.

By recess, Sarah seemed to be okay. She laughed and played jump rope as if nothing had happened.

Alex was still disturbed. People he didn't know, dying in a plane crash—that was sad. Sarah's reaction to it was horrific. He thought about what he had told her.

You can't let that sadness live in your mind. You'll go crazy.

He decided that sadness would never control him. Instead, he would control sadness.

That's how it started. He never truly felt sadness again.

He never got angry, *really* angry, until fourth grade.

There was this big kid, Ronald Something, who was a grade ahead. Everyone called him Big Ron. There was something wrong with him. He was already taller than two of the lady teachers. He had been held back once or twice and should've been in middle school. And he was mean. Big Ron made trouble for anyone smaller and weaker than he was. He developed a particular dislike for Alex and started picking on him.

This consisted of the usual elementary school shenanigans—tripping, body slamming, and noogies. Alex shrugged it off at first, but the bullying got worse. Alex complained to his teacher, who listened sympathetically but seemed powerless to help. Alex's mother was supportive and wrote a letter to the principal.

Despite this, the bullying increased and became unbearable.

One day, Big Ron shoved Alex hard. Alex fell to the floor and skidded another ten feet down the hall—

—then he was in the waiting room of the principal's office. He was banged up and sore. He held a bloody washcloth. Tears poured from his eyes. Snot and blood were dripping from his nose. Big Ron must have beat him up.

He heard his mother's voice beyond the office door. She and the principal were having a discussion.

"What are we going to do about this?" the principal asked. "That boy's in the hospital."

Someone was in the hospital?

"I gave you plenty of time to nip it in the bud," Mother said. "Did you do anything?"

"I've contacted the parents a number of times. I had a meeting with them last week. They weren't helpful." There was a pause. "They're threatening to sue."

"Sue whom?"

"The school district. You and Mr. Herman."

Mother laughed. "Are the incidents with the other students documented ?" she asked.

"Of course. It's not my first rodeo," the principal said.

"I'm willing to compromise. Let's set up weekly sessions with the district social worker."

"For Alex or Ronald?"

"Both. Ronald clearly needs counseling, and it wouldn't hurt Alex. If that doesn't pacify the parents, use the prior incidents for leverage," Mother said. "Tell them we'll countersue if they don't back off. That should do it."

There was a pause as the principal considered this.

"Okay," the principal said.

"One more thing," Mother said. "Suspend Alex for a week. It'll look good to the kid's parents, and Alex could use some time away from all this drama."

"Done," the principal said.

Alex loved his mother. She understood him.

The week at home went by quickly. His mother took a week of personal time from her teaching job. Alex spent much of the time reading.

On his first day back at school, some kids looked at Alex strangely. But one kid looked at him with admiration.

"What's with you?" Alex asked him.

The kid smiled and shook his head. "You and Big Ron. It was the coolest thing I ever saw."

"What exactly happened?"

"You don't remember?"

"No. Not at all."

"You went berserk! It took four teachers to pull you off of him! He was bleeding so much that everyone thought he was dead!"

Alex didn't like hearing this. He hated Big Ron, but the thought he had caused pain to another creature was disturbing.

After lunch, he had to meet with the social worker, a young lady named Ms. Jackson. He was worried that she would think he was some kind of monster, the kind of kid who liked to fight. But she was nice to him.

On the first day, they talked about what had happened. She seemed to know more about the incident than he did.

"I don't remember the fight," he said. "Am I crazy?"

"Oh, heavens no," she said. "You dissociated. That happens sometimes when something really bad happens to a person. Their mind blocks it out as a sort of self-protection strategy."

She told him what kind of behavior was expected of him. These things he already knew. Ms. Jackson repeated the lecture he had gotten from his mother.

"Bullies are unfortunate," she told him, "but everyone comes across them from time to time. You're a good kid, Alex, but you have to control your emotions."

"Like Mr. Spock on Star Trek."

"Yep. Exactly."

The takeaway message was, "Control your emotions, control your emotions." Alex's obsessive-compulsive disorder kicked in to ensure his emotional control was successful. He could do anything if he had the support of his OCD.

He enjoyed his Monday sessions with Ms. Jackson. He liked her. When he entered her room, she'd say, "Good afternoon, Alex! How are you today?"

"Just fine, Ms. Jackson, and yourself?"

"Just peachy. Is there anything you'd like to talk about?"

"No, not really. May I read?"

"Yes, you may, Alex. Thanks for asking so politely."

Alex sometimes wondered whatever happened to Big Ron, whether he lived, whether he died, or whether he lived and was permanently disabled. Big Ron never came back to school, at least not *that* school.

That was a mixed blessing. Alex never had to deal with him again.

What he *did* have to deal with was the guilt, the doubts about his mental health, and the voice in his head saying, "Control your emotions, control your emotions."

So he learned to do just that. The voice went silent when the programming was complete.

Sadness: check.

Anger: double-check.

Chapter 14

THE POPE RUNS OUT OF MONEY

On the first day of seventh grade, there were a lot of new students. There were so many that the middle school had to borrow chairs from the community center to tide them over until new desks could come in.

"Where did all these kids come from?" Alex asked.

"Saint Thomas Catholic closed down," said Sarah Barnette. She was Catholic. Her parents weren't wealthy enough to send her to Catholic school, but she went to the same church as the students of Saint Thomas, so she had inside information. "My dad says the Pope ran out of money."

"How is that even possible?"

"I don't know."

The boys from Saint Thomas were like all of the other boys. The girls, though—they were charming. Their manners were impeccable. They were angelic, as though they were channeling The Blessed Virgin Mary.

That year they showed a couple of videos. One was on puberty and the changes that came with it. The other was about reproduction and its perils—pregnancy, sexually transmitted diseases, depression, and social isolation if things went badly. The videos did a great job of describing things without giving any details. They separated the boys and girls so they could ask questions less awkwardly—a good idea, in theory. Alex had plenty of questions but was too self-conscious to ask them.

He started growing hair in places he'd never grown it before. His behavior was changing, and there wasn't anything he could do about it.

Like with Sarah Barnette. They'd been friends since kindergarten, but things were becoming...different. He felt anxious around her. By Christmas, he couldn't even talk to her. Every time he tried, his mind froze up for no good reason. The friendship withered, and he mourned the loss.

Alex noticed that his peers were changing, too. The girls giggled and played with their hair more.

The boys got even stupider and angrier. It reminded him of something he'd read about the elderly. It was obvious what was happening— the males were getting dementia.

One night at dinner, an awful thought came to him. His intellect was the only good thing he had. What if he lost that? It was too horrible to think about. But he thought about it anyway.

"Do you suppose..." he said, stopped, and thought some more. "Is it possible that testosterone kills brain cells?" he asked.

His father laughed.

His mother smiled and said, "No, dear. It only seems that way."

The next day, his mother took him to the library, and they checked out some books: The Joy of Sex, The Sensuous Man, Everything You Ever Wanted to Know About Sex, etcetera. These books were written for adults. They had important details in them that the videos in school had left out. Alex devoured them. It turned out that the universe was more wonderful and bizarre than Alex could have imagined.

His mind was blown.

Chapter 15

THE NEW KID

The high school got a new student on the first day of ninth grade. This guy was handsome and the teenage equivalent of suave. The girls practically swooned when they met him. He was all they could talk about for a while.

The story was that he was from California, Beverly Hills, to be exact. Rumor had it that his father was a lawyer, his mother a psychiatrist. He had a motorcycle, even though he didn't have his driver's license yet.

Most intriguing was the rumor that the new kid knew kung fu. All the stories turned out to be true, more or less.

One day, at the end of lunch, Alex went to the boys' room to drain his bladder before the next class. Two members of the football team, notorious bullies, were there when Alex walked in. He walked up to a urinal and unzipped his jeans.

"Hey, Herman!" one of them said. "Where's the ten dollars you owe me?" The other one snickered.

Alex didn't owe anyone money. He dreaded what was coming. He finished urinating, zipped his jeans, and began to wash his hands.

"I'm talking to you, freak!"

Alex reached for a paper towel. The bully spun him around and pushed him against the wall.

They heard the door to the boys' room open.

"Hello, men." It was the new kid. "What are we up to?"

"Just giving the nerd a hard time," said the first.

"Yeah," said the second. "We were about to give him a swirly."

"What fun!" said the new kid. "I'm in! Let's make it interesting—whatever you do to him, I'm going to do to you." He stood there and smiled calmly, confidently, without a trace of anger or animosity.

The first bully scowled and let go of Alex. He took two steps toward the new kid, and—Alex didn't exactly see what happened. It was all a blur. But in an instant, the bully flew backward, hit the wall hard, and rode it down to the floor.

The new kid smiled. "Oops," he said.

"I'm gonna kick your ass!" said the bully.

"Lying on the floor? I don't think so."

The bully groaned and slowly got to his feet.

The new kid looked at the other bully. "Were you about to say something?"

The other one shook his head.

"Well, off you go, men. I have private business with the nerd."

They left.

"That was fun," said the new kid. He extended his hand. "Brad Tucker."

Alex shook it. "Alex Herman."

"I know. I hear you're pretty good at math." Alex nodded humbly. "My grades in trig are sub-par," Brad said. "I need to bring them up. What do you say to some tutoring?"

"I don't know."

"My folks will pay. And they'll pay well."

"Can I think it over?"

"Sure. Take some time." He handed Alex a business card. "But don't take too long. You're my first choice, but I do have a list. Nice meeting you. See you around." Brad turned and left.

Alex looked at the card in his hand. It had Brad's name and contact information. And he thought, *What high school freshman has his own business cards?*

A couple of days later, Alex made his decision. And why not? He wasn't doing anything so important that he couldn't help out another human being. He called the number on the card.

"Tucker residence," a woman said.

"Dr. Tucker? This is Alex Herman. Brad asked if I'd tutor him in trig. I'd like to give it a shot."

"Excellent," she said. "Could you come after dinner tonight? We should get to know each other before we commit to anything."

He told his mom and dad where he was going at dinner, and they approved. Alex had no close friends, so they always supported him when he had a reason to leave the house.

The Tuckers lived within cycling distance, and Alex found himself at the Tuckers' front door in a few minutes.

When Dr. Tucker answered the door, Alex introduced himself but couldn't look her in the eye. He'd been practicing but couldn't always do it.

"Well, come in! We're going to talk in the family room. Would you like a piece of apple pie? Glass of milk?"

He followed her into the house. "Yes to the pie. No beverage, thank you."

Brad and his father were waiting in the family room.

"Hey, amigo," Brad said.

Brad's father stood and extended his hand. "Bill Tucker."

Alex shook his hand.

"Pleased to meet you."

"Have a seat."

Mrs. Tucker brought in the dessert and sat.

"This is like an interview," she said, "but I don't want you to feel any anxiety. Brad speaks highly of you. He needs to get his grades up, and we want to make sure this is a good fit."

"Okay. Ask away."

"What do your parents do for a living?"

"My father's a mechanical engineer. My mother teaches first grade."

"What's your GPA?"

"Four point 0, so far." He crossed his fingers.

"Very good. What extracurricular activities are you involved in?"

"Chess club."

"That's it?"

"Yes, ma'am."

"No sports?"

"No, ma'am. Never got interested."

"What do you do for fun?"

"I read. And I dabble in electronics."

"Very good. Do you have a girlfriend?"

Alex got self-conscious. “No, ma’am. I have friends that are girls, but I’m not dating.”

“Fair enough. Now I want you to be honest with this one: do you do drugs?”

“Charlotte!” said Mr. Tucker.

“Mom!” said Brad.

“We have to be careful who we let into our lives.”

“It’s okay,” Alex said. “The answer is no. I’ve never been tempted. I don’t have a lot of friends. I don’t get invited to those kinds of parties.”

She smiled sympathetically. “Don’t worry, Alex. You’ll find your stride. One more question—do you know anything about autism?” she asked. She was, after all, a psychiatrist.

He knew about autism. He had suspected he was on the spectrum as soon as he found out there *was* a spectrum. But he had learned to be skeptical of his imagination because there were so many interesting diseases. It was exhausting. At times in his life, he’d thought he had OCD, a fear that had some basis; five different types of cancer; schizophrenia; Lyme disease; and others too numerous to mention. It had almost made him give up reading medical journals. The only thing he was sure of was that he was a hypochondriac.

He didn’t say all of that. “I haven’t been formally diagnosed,” he told her.

“If you’re autistic, you’re very high-functioning. That makes it harder to diagnose. Maybe you’re just an introvert. We can work with you on that. I wouldn’t worry. You’re going to be okay. Our Brad is dyslexic.”

“Thus, the need for a tutor,” Brad said.

“Do you feel disabled, Brad?”

“Not at all.”

“How’s your life?”

"Awesome, and getting better every day."

"We all have issues," Mrs. Tucker continued, "things that seem to be problems. It's how we deal with them that determines how good our lives are going to be. Well, Alex—I think this is going to be a great fit."

They worked out a schedule: Saturday afternoon, from 1 to five, with a break in the middle. The Tuckers offered Alex a generous ten dollars an hour at a time when the state minimum wage was $3.35.

Brad was a good pupil. He couldn't read well, but he was motivated, had a good memory, and was good at retaining auditory information. And it turned out that his failure in trig was due to one thing: his mind was so locked onto the Cartesian system that he couldn't grasp polar coordinates. Once they broke through that barrier, everything came easily.

After three Saturdays, Alex said Brad didn't need his help anymore. Alex offered to tender his resignation.

"Why would you want to give up a cake job like this?" Brad asked him.

"I think it's the right thing to do."

"Maybe you think too much."

Alex would hear those words many times over the course of his life.

That was the beginning of their friendship—a boys' room brawl and Saturday tutoring sessions. Brad was the first close friend Alex had ever had.

Alex started spending a lot of time at Brad's house, even when he wasn't tutoring. Studying, playing video games, and the occasional one-on-one at the basketball hoop in front of the Tucker garage. He liked Brad's parents, and they liked him. Mrs. Tucker helped Alex navigate the difficulties of being a young man with no social skills.

Alex told Mrs. Tucker about the problem he had talking to girls.

"I know a trick that might help," she said. "Find someplace quiet where you won't be disturbed. Find a picture of a girl you're attracted to, and talk to the picture out loud. Pretend you're having real conversations on a variety of topics. You have to be alone, so no one will think you're crazy. Smile, relax, and, most importantly, focus on the eyes. All it takes is time and practice. When you've practiced with pictures, and you've built your confidence, you can graduate to a real girl."

"Does that really work?" It sounded too easy.

"It worked for Brad. I'm sure it'll work for you."

Chapter 16

IMAGINARY GIRLFRIEND

His peers started to pair up. Alex felt left out.

For Alex, girls came in two varieties—female friends and Other. Girls that were his friends were like him—nerdy, bookish, and socially inept outside their small circle. He liked these girls. He was comfortable with them and could have conversations without stuttering, blushing, or being clumsy. The problem was he wasn't attracted to the girls that were his friends.

Then there were the girls who had transformed, like Sarah Barnette. They had become Other.

The sad thing was he couldn't talk to Other without stammering. It bordered on tragedy. He was awkward even with the super-nice Catholic girls—they would tolerate him and be polite, but you could tell they had set loftier goals. Being brides of Jesus, or the star football player, maybe. He couldn't compete with Christ or quarterbacks.

During that semester, Alex found a Sears catalog in the living room. He took it to his room to see what it had in the way of school supplies and educational toys. He met his first crush there, about one-third from the beginning, in the lingerie section.

She was Other.

She was about thirty years old, doe-eyed, with large breasts and auburn hair. She must have been a popular model. There were quite a few pictures of her, usually in a bra and panties, but sometimes in pajamas, sometimes in a flannel nightgown, or a slip. She was beautiful, no matter what she was wearing. She looked sweet. She looked intelligent. She looked like she'd be a good mother.

He imagined a biography for her. She was Catholic and of Irish descent. He gave her a name—Kathleen. Her last name was Sears, because he met her in the Sears catalog.

There were obstacles, to be sure. The age difference was substantial. And the fact that she was only a collection of pictures in a catalog. But he could talk to her.

In Alex's fantasy, she would wait for him to get older. He would go to college and become an engineer or physicist, something that made a good living. He would buy her a beautiful house to raise their family in.

Here's how they would make love:

Alex would lie in bed, hold the catalog on his belly with his left hand, and touch himself with his right.

Alex would say, "*Hello, Kathleen. You're looking beautiful today.*"

"*Why, thank you, my handsome man.*"

"*I've been counting the minutes.*"

"Me, too."

"I'd like to make love to you."

"Yes, but I'm a good Catholic girl. We must wait until we're bound by the holy sacrament of marriage."

"I know. Do you mind if I look at you while I...?"

"No, not at all. You have needs. Your happiness is important to me."

When he was done, he'd look her in the eyes for a while and say, "*I have to go now.*"

"I know. See you soon."

He'd kiss her picture, close the catalog, and slide it under his bed.

Wait for me, Kathleen, he'd tell her.

You're being ridiculous, he'd tell himself.

He sometimes wondered if he was insane.

Chapter 17

MARCI WEBER

After Dr.Tucker taught him the technique, Alex practiced a lot with his fantasy woman. He looked at her eyes more often and her body less often. His practice conversations became more relaxed and intimate. Dr. Tucker was right. He was gaining confidence.

One day during the fall of eleventh grade, he decided he was ready to ask a real girl for a date.

Sarah Barnette was out of the question now. She was always going steady with someone and had a waiting list of potential suitors.

He chose Marci Weber. They had been friends ever since seventh grade. She, like him, had been a socially awkward nerd.

That was in the past. Over the previous summer, she had become Other. She wasn't skinny anymore, having gained weight in her buttocks and chest. Her torso narrowed at the waist and gracefully widened at the hips. Her horned-rim glasses were gone, and instead of the baggy sweaters and jeans she used to wear, her clothes now hugged her figure.

Why did these things make a difference? Alex didn't know, but they did. It didn't make any sense. That was something even the books on sexuality couldn't tell him.

Alex sat across from Marci at lunch one day.

"Hi, Marci," he said. "Haven't seen you at chess club lately." Success! He didn't stammer.

"I know. I've been crazy busy."

He got right to the point before he could chicken out. "Would you like to go to homecoming with me?" he asked.

She smiled. "Gee, that's sweet of you to ask, but I already have a date."

He wasn't too disappointed. He knew it had been a long shot. "Maybe some other time, then."

"I don't know when. I'm booked up until Christmas break. Gotta fit in time to study."

"Gee, you're popular all of a sudden."

"Yeah," she said. "I don't get it. But I'm taking advantage of the situation." She leaned in close and whispered, "I made out with a guy for the first time Saturday Night. It was awesome."

"Anybody I know?"

"Probably not. A jock from Dexter. He doesn't have much going on between the ears, but he's really cute. I'm having a lot of fun. I really like making out."

"I think I'd like it too."

"You're a good guy. Your time's coming."

As rejections go, it wasn't bad.

Chapter 18

COLLEGE

Alex graduated high school third in his class. Marci Weber was valedictorian. Sarah Barnette was salutatorian. They had taken more advanced placement courses than he had. He didn't mind. It meant he didn't have to give a speech on graduation day.

He was accepted into the University of Michigan's School of Engineering.

Brad's GPA was near the top of the class, not good enough to get into Harvard, but good enough for the business school at the U of M. It would do.

Brad got his bachelor's in business in the typical four years. He didn't pursue a master's. He was eager to start a career.

It took Alex an extra year to get his bachelor's because he made a course correction during his junior year. While on the University's solar car team, he met a computer science major named Larry Page, who would go on to start a company called Google. Larry got Alex excited about the possibilities of the internet, so Alex changed his major to computer science. Most of his credits crossed over, but some of them didn't.

Then Lollapalooza happened.

Chapter 19
LOLLAPALOOZA

Two interesting things happened on July 24th, 1994. Alex discovered the principles of a useful search engine and met his future wife. Well, sort of.

Brad had bought two weekend passes to Lollapalooza but suddenly found himself without a girlfriend, so he gave the extra ticket to Alex.

Alex picked up Brad at his apartment early in the morning. Brad insisted on leaving at nine am because the traffic going into the venue, Pine Knob, would be brutal.

He was right. Traffic on the expressway got congested three miles before their exit.

Brad lit a joint.

"Can't it wait until we get to the parking lot?"

"I've got another one for the parking lot." He offered the joint to Alex, who shook his head.

"This traffic is insane," said Alex.

"That's why we left so early. Last year, I missed Alice in Chains. The whole set."

Forty-five minutes later, a parking attendant finally guided them into a space in the lot. Brad fired up another joint, took a hit, and offered it to Alex. Alex looked around to make sure no cops were waiting to swoop in.

A dozen cars around them had occupants smoking weed, so he figured it was safe. He took the joint from Brad and took a hit.

He coughed. He frowned.

"You look tense," Brad said, "What's on your mind?"

"The solar car project I'm working on. We're having trouble getting components."

"Why is that?"

"We know the parts are out there, but we don't know where or how to get them."

"That's what faculty advisors are for."

"They don't have a clue, either. We're trying to develop cutting-edge technology, and we're stymied."

"How about this internet thing?" Brad seemed to think that the internet was an all-knowing oracle when actually it was a lot of hard work and frequently just a distraction.

"Sure, but the problem is search engines. They're weak. The best one is Webcrawler, and it sucks."

"You lost me."

"The results are practically random. Random results are useless."

"I still don't understand. Maybe you could explain it to me someday. I'm too stoned right now." He looked at his watch. "We should head in. Mouth's dry. I need beer."

They left the car and headed to the entrance of the venue.

"Do you think there's going to be real money in the internet?" Brad asked. "Business opportunities?"

"Yeah, but the question is when?" Alex said. "I just heard about a startup called Amazon."

"What do they do?"

"Online bookseller."

"That sounds like a bad business model," Brad said. "Do you think it'll work?"

"I don't see how," Alex said. "I checked out their website the other night. It was kind of cool, but it took five minutes to load their landing page."

"Someday, I'll figure out a way to harness that brain of yours, and we'll be billionaires."

They filtered through the entrance, where security checked everyone for weapons and other contraband.

Brad looked at his watch again. "An hour before they start. I'm going for beer. Stay right here."

Alex sat on a low wall that contained a flower bed. He felt mellow. The marijuana had loosened the shackles of his mind, but he hadn't had enough to make him stupid.

The problem with search engines: Webcrawler was a good start, but it was as if they'd stopped in the middle of the development process. Even Larry Page was having a hard time with it. And that guy was brilliant. They needed a way to prioritize the results.

What if you could somehow give weight to more recent pages? And weight to more popular pages? Maybe a few simple lines of code, tracking incoming links.

And like magic, the lines of code appeared in his mind.

How would you generate revenue? There would have to be a way to pay for all of this. Advertising?

I hope I can remember all this the next time I see Larry.

Alex snapped out of his reverie. Brad was handing him a red plastic cup full of beer.

"Looks like you've made some friends." Brad pointed across the walk opposite them.

Alex realized he was staring in the direction of a beautiful woman—about his age, with blond hair, blue eyes, and a fantastic figure barely contained by a tank top and cut-off jeans.

The blonde's female companion glared at him and gave him the finger. She thought he'd been staring at *them,* when he'd really been looking into the future of the search engine.

Alex was stoned enough to forget that he was awkward and shy. He smiled and waved. The companion stood, pulled the woman to her feet, and led her away. He looked at them as they walked off.

But the blonde looked back. Alex waved again.

Wow, he said to himself. *What just happened?*

"Look at you," Brad said. "Getting friendly with a babe."

Alex shrugged. "I'm a little high," he said.

"You're welcome," Brad said.

Alex had a great time at Lollapalooza, but the highlight of the day was the blond woman, the one he'd never seen before and would likely never see again. He thought about her every day.

Alex had to take an art appreciation class to fulfill his humanities requirements. He had waited until his final year to take it. It had slipped his mind until the graduation audit with his academic advisor. It was a mandatory distraction from his real interests.

He sat in an empty lecture hall as students filtered in, and someone behind him said, "Did you enjoy Lollapalooza?"

He turned his head—it was the beautiful blonde. What were the chances?

"I enjoyed it very much," he said.

He smiled and offered the seat next to him. Her name was Lucy. After class, she walked with him to the student union, where they drank coffee and talked. Over the next few weeks, he offered lunch, movie tickets, and his bed.

Lucy was Other, but she became a friend. She eventually edged Brad out to become his *best* friend. She accepted all of his quirks but didn't seem to have any quirks of her own. He thought he was dating out of his league, but she assured him he wasn't.

Alex and Lucy were virgins when they met. He got to try the knowledge from the books he'd read in seventh grade. They learned together.

They never discussed sharing a living space. It happened naturally, organically. Lucy was living in the cramped room of a dormitory. Alex had a large apartment overlooking the Huron River. It had a balcony with a lovely view. Lucy would visit with a bookbag full of sketch pads and pencils and an overnight bag with a change of clothes. She frequently spent the night. They'd study together, read, or make love.

One morning, Alex opened the bottom drawer of his dresser. It was full of women's underwear and socks.

"What's this?" he asked.

Lucy looked anxious. "I didn't think you'd mind. It's more convenient if I have some things here."

He nodded. He went to the walk-in closet and opened the door. He looked inside and pondered. There was plenty of room.

"Which side of the closet would you like?" he asked.

She smiled.

"It doesn't matter," she said.

He nodded again.

"Okay. You can have the right side."

He hung his Dockers and polo shirts on the left.

"There," he said.

She started crying. She stood, hugged him hard, and showered him with kisses.

"Oh, thank you! Thank you!" she said.

Such big emotions over such a little thing, he thought. He didn't get it. But she was happy, and that made him happy.

She moved the rest of her belongings the following week, and just like that, they were living together. It was almost too easy.

Eventually, he offered her a wedding ring, a house, and a child.

She politely accepted all of it.

Chapter 20

A MISSED OPPORTUNITY

In 1998, Alex got a job with a software contractor applying fixes for the Y2K bug. The company's clients were corporations and government agencies, large and small. The world was losing its mind over Y2K. That meant jobs were good, and the pay was generous. He reported to a project manager who was easy to get along with. He had minimal contact with other people. He liked the work and loved the money. He'd been out of school only three years and already had a six-figure salary.

What he didn't like was traveling. The job required flying, and a lot of it. Flying gave Alex panic attacks. But he made enough money to feel financially secure.

He asked Lucy to marry him, and she said yes. They bought a house and talked about having children.

When Google launched, Alex got a call from Larry Page. Google was going to be big, Larry said. He offered Alex a job on the coveted ground floor.

"How will you make money?" Alex asked.

"Advertising," Larry said.

"But how?" Alex wanted to know.

"We haven't worked out the details."

Alex turned him down. Nobody had ever made serious money from a search engine.

A crystal ball would have come in handy at the time.

Brad would remind Alex once in a while when he felt like being a prick.

"When opportunity comes knockin'," he'd say, "Alex Herman runs and hides in the basement."

Which had some truth to it.

It all worked to Brad's advantage, though. In 2000, when he finally saw the potential of the internet, he talked Alex into starting a business with him. That became Tucker-Herman Web Services.

They didn't become billionaires, but they did okay.

Chapter 21

TERMINAL LACK OF ENTHUSIASM

Lucy had never met anyone like Alex. He was sensitive, thoughtful, and kind. When he was focused on something, he had an intensity she found appealing. He had quirks and faults, but his good qualities outweighed the bad.

Plenty of guys had given her attention in high school, mostly unwanted. She had a face and body that the boys found attractive. It was both a blessing and a curse. It was obvious what they were after, and she had no use for them. Alex was the first male ever to get *her* attention. She had never known what she was looking for in a partner, but after they met, she realized he was it.

Lucy had a melancholy disposition. It never crossed her mind that this was unhealthy until Hannah was born. Lucy had been over the moon while pregnant, but after they came home from the hospital, something wasn't right. The melancholy came back, now magnified. After a few weeks of unbearable sadness, her doctor diagnosed her with postpartum depression. The doctor prescribed an antidepressant, and Lucy started feeling better.

After six months, she felt well enough to be weaned off the meds. She settled into healthy motherhood.

But when Hannah started kindergarten, the house began to feel empty in those few hours when Hannah was at school. Lucy saw how this would go—full days of first grade, the rest of public school, then college, a career, and marriage. Hannah was sure to be moving away, out of their lives. What would Lucy have then? Alex. Would he be enough? She didn't think so.

Some days were good. On those days, the melancholy didn't make sense. She had a good life and everything it took to be happy. On the bad days, she wondered what it would be like to simply not exist.

What was the point of it all?

She didn't contemplate harming herself at first. But eventually, she thought about it a lot.

One day, before she got Hannah up for school, the depression hit hard. She couldn't get out of bed. She curled into a ball and started crying.

Alex was getting ready for work.

"What's the matter, baby?" Alex asked her.

"I don't know, I don't know!"

He asked her if she was in pain. She nodded. When he asked her where it hurt, she pointed to her head and her heart.

"Okay, okay." He kissed her on the head. "We're going to get you some help."

He got her dressed and took Hannah next door to Mrs. Rossetti.

When they got to the ER, Lucy was too incapacitated to walk. Alex had to get her into a wheelchair and push her to the admissions desk.

When the triage nurse asked Lucy if she had been having thoughts of hurting herself, she covered her eyes, nodded, and wept uncontrollably.

They prescribed the same antidepressant she took to this day and kept her for observation for a week. By the following weekend, it was as if nothing had happened. Everything was fine, and they let her come home.

The antidepressant did what it was supposed to. Alex and Lucy were both relieved. It went that way for about twelve years. Life was good, mostly. She was married to a good man, lived in a lovely house, and had a daughter she loved to the moon and back.

Once in a while, she'd wonder if there wasn't something more. But the sadness was never severe, and it would pass. Alex made enough money to make them comfortable, so she didn't need a real job. She had been an art major in college, but now being a wife and mother was her art. She filled her days with cooking and housework, the occasional PTO meeting, and exercise classes.

She was surprised and delighted when she met Kay. She had a neighbor her age! Lucy was eager to know her better.

Kay was unique. She laughed a lot and smiled even more. She had an outrageous sense of humor and no filter controlling the things she said. She was playful, witty, full of energy, and beautiful.

Kay was all the things Lucy wanted to be.

Chapter 22

TREEHOUSE REVISITED

"I've always wanted to see the inside," said Lucy.

Lucy and Kay looked up at the treehouse while their husbands were getting to know each other.

"Well, here's your chance," said Kay. She climbed the ladder. When she reached the top, she pushed open the trap door and climbed inside. "Come on up!"

Lucy climbed and stuck her head inside. She waited for her eyes to adjust to the dim light before climbing in.

Mr. Rossetti had been a carpenter before he retired, so the structure was well made. There was a lawn chair, a dead flashlight, a moldy army cot, and a footlocker secured with a padlock.

"I like it," Kay said. She stuck her head out the window. "Hey, Frank! I can see our house from up here!"

Lucy laughed. She went to the footlocker and examined the lock. "I wonder what's in here?"

"We'll find out. I had a lock-picking class when I went to ninja school." Lucy snickered. "But all my good burglar tools are in the garage, buried under Frank's golf paraphernalia."

Lucy laughed again.

"Well, I've seen enough," Kay said. "There's work to do, but not tonight. We have a lot of wine, and it's not going to drink itself."

They climbed down to the ground. As they passed the pool, Kay stuck a toe in the water and said, "I don't know. Tell me what you think."

Lucy went to the edge, slipped the sandal off her foot, and stuck her toe in. She knew it was coming. She had only known Kay for a few hours, but she already *knew* her. Lucy took a deep breath as Kay raised her hand to push her into the pool. In a fraction of a second, Lucy knew that she would pretend to be drowning, and make Kay worry about her for a few seconds, then she would pull Kay in with her. Surprise! And—

And life was good again. Not just good, but *really* good.

Chapter 23
BONDING

The next day, Kay took Lucy shopping. They were a good team—Lucy knew where the good shops were, and Kay had a credit card with an infinite limit.

First, they tried on swimsuits. Lucy picked out a modest one-piece and tried it on. When she came out of the fitting room, Kay frowned.

"It's frumpy," Kay said.

"I don't want anything too racy."

"The whole point of a swimsuit is to display the goods without revealing everything. You've got the body of a goddess. You should show it off."

Kay found a string bikini Lucy's size, handed it to her, and pushed her toward the fitting room.

Lucy put the swimsuit on and looked at herself in the mirror. Kay was right. She *was* beautiful. She stepped out of the fitting room to get Kay's opinion.

"There you go," Kay said. They paid for it with Kay's credit card.

They took a break for lunch. They sipped on coffee while waiting for their salads.

"Tell me a secret," Kay said. Lucy was puzzled. "It's a bonding thing women do when they're getting to know each other."

Lucy paused to think. "I take an antidepressant," she eventually said.

"Good God, who doesn't? I was hoping for something juicier than that. Okay, you have depression. Why?"

"I don't know. It always seemed that something was missing, and I could never figure out what."

"Is the antidepressant working for you?"

Lucy shrugged. "It's kept me alive."

"If something's missing in my life, I figure it out and get it. I've heard it affects your libido. True?"

"Sex was never a big thing with me. Now I'm pretty much dead from the waist down."

"I'm sad for you. How does Alex feel about your, um, lack of desire?"

"I try to make him happy. No complaints so far."

"Did you ever figure out what was missing?"

"I don't even think about it anymore. It's not important."

Kay frowned as she sipped her coffee.

"Your turn," Lucy said. "Tell me a secret."

"Okay. I'm an expert at reading people."

"Pshaw."

"What are you, my grandmother? It's true. It's my superpower. I'm never wrong."

"Okay. What are you reading about me?"

Kay looked her in the eye. "You know what's missing in your life. It's right there. You just have to dig a little."

That made Lucy uncomfortable. There was an awkward pause. What Kay said sounded like the truth and, at the same time, a schtick from a carnival fortune teller.

"Well, you're a disappointment," Lucy said. "You're wrong."

"There's a first time for everything."

"Also, not very juicy."

"I agree, not juicy." Kay pondered. "Okay. I've got something you might call juicy, but you have to promise not to tell anyone."

"I promise."

"Cross your heart?" Lucy crossed her heart. "Frank and I have an open marriage."

Lucy's jaw dropped. "What do you mean?"

"You know—polyamorous. Non-monogamous."

Lucy couldn't believe her ears.

"I'm a slut," Kay said proudly.

"You sleep with other men?"

"On occasion, I have sex with other men. It rarely involves sleep."

"And Frank's okay with that?"

"He has to be. I had conditions when I accepted his proposal. That was one. He does what he wants, and I do what I want. We're married. We don't own each other."

"Wow."

"Make no mistake—I really love that old man. I'll take care of him as long as he's alive. But I am what I am, and it has to be this way. There's no lying or guilt. Everything's honest and upfront."

Lucy didn't know what to say.

"Do you think I'm a pervert?" Kay said.

"No, not at all. It's different, is all. I've never met anyone that was... polyamorous."

"You'd be surprised. We don't advertise. You need to be careful if you want a social life. I told *you* because I know you'll keep the secret. And you should know. You and I are going to be best friends."

"I feel honored."

On the way back to the car, they passed a kiosk where two men were taking donations to help Ukrainian refugees.

Kay opened her purse and put a couple of bills in their donation jar.

"Stay strong, men! I'm on your side!" she said.

Lucy put a $20 bill in their jar, too.

The men thanked them in English. As they walked away, the older one said something in a language Lucy took to be Ukrainian. Whatever he said, the younger man seemed to agree.

Kay turned and said something in the same language. The men looked at each other in surprise and burst out laughing. The older man nodded and said, "Yes, very nice," in English.

"What was that all about?" Lucy asked when they were further down the sidewalk.

"The old guy said, 'The blonde's got a nice caboose."

Lucy blushed. "And what did you say?" she asked.

"I said, 'What am I, chopped liver?'"

Lucy laughed.

"You know Ukrainian?" she asked.

"Oh! I guess I do." Kay acted as if it was a surprise to her, too.

"Just how many languages do you know?" Lucy asked.

"I don't know. I lost count." Lucy couldn't tell if she was joking.

She thought about sharing Kay's secret with Alex but didn't know how he'd react. He wasn't very open-minded sometimes. Besides, Lucy had been sworn to secrecy.

She decided to honor Kay's wishes.

She returned home with the bags of clothes she had bought. She had the urge to make love. It was peculiar. She pretended to feel desire sometimes because it pleased Alex, but she hadn't really felt that way in years. Now she was eager.

She went up the stairs with seduction on her mind, thinking how happy it would make him. But he was in so much pain that he actually turned down sex. The poor man couldn't catch a break.

Chapter 24

THE ORACLE

After Lucy had her morning coffee, she went next door to see Kay.

"Hey, girlfriend. Come on in."

"I came over to help you settle in," Lucy said.

"No need. I worked through the night. Just finishing up."

To Lucy's surprise, the house was organized already. The pieces of furniture had all found their places. The dishes and cookware had all been put away. What should have taken days had been done in one night.

Kay walked to the infamous cabinet that had wrecked Alex's back. In front of it was a wooden crate full of curios. Kay removed one, a figurine of a nude woman, wiped it with a cloth, and placed it on a shelf.

"Wow," Lucy said. "That's an interesting piece. It reminds me of the Venus of Brassempouy. Only this one's intact. The real one is in pieces."

"I'm careful when I move."

"Can I see it?"

Kay handed the figurine to her. Lucy turned it around and examined every detail.

"I was an art major. This piece is fabulous."

"I dated the artist for a while. He was talented."

Kay pulled out another, done in the Classical Greek style. The woman's breasts were small, while her derriere was ample, as was the fashion in those days. "I modeled for this one. For the record, my ass has never been this big. I think the sculptor needed glasses."

"But the detail...they look authentic."

Kay continued her work. "I've got an appointment with a psychic in a little bit," she said. "Want to come along?"

"Sure," Lucy said.

Kay carefully wiped the remaining pieces and placed them on the shelves.

The psychic did business in a building that was an oddity. It was an old house in the middle of the city's commercial district, surrounded by shops and office buildings.

They walked up the creaking steps to the front door. Kay rang the buzzer. A woman in her sixties opened the door. She had gray hair and bright blue eyes. The woman smiled.

"We're your one o'clock," Kay said.

"Won't you come in?" the woman said, with an accent that reminded Lucy of the fortune teller in a horror movie. "Right this way." She led them to a parlor that smelled of sage and patchouli. A circular table took up the center of the room, covered with a cloth adorned with astrological symbols. "I see there are two of you."

"Two readings," Kay said. "I'll pay for both."

The woman nodded. "Please sit. Would you like some tea?"

"Yes, please."

"I will be right back," the woman said. She returned with two steaming cups.

"Who would like to go first?" the woman asked.

"Me," said Kay.

"Very well." The woman picked up a deck of Tarot cards and drew one—the Tower.

Kay and the woman looked at each other solemnly.

"What does that mean?" Lucy asked.

"Let us wait until all the cards are drawn before we interpret meaning," the woman said. "Shall I go on?" Kay nodded. The woman drew The Death Card—the Grim Reaper. Even Lucy knew what that one meant.

The woman drew the remaining cards required for the reading. Lucy was so disturbed that she couldn't pay attention, even though she felt it was all nonsense.

"Well?" the woman said.

Kay said, "There aren't any surprises here. I just wanted some clarity."

"You have knowledge of the Tarot," the woman said, "so you know these things are not written in stone."

Kay nodded. "Lucy's turn."

"Very well." The woman shuffled the deck. "Are we ready?"

"Lay it on me," Lucy said.

The woman drew The Fool. She drew The Empress and laid it down to The Fool's right. She started a new row with the death card.

Lucy stiffened. Kay touched her on the thigh. "Relax. It's not what you think."

The Ten of Swords was drawn and laid down to the right of Death. The final card drawn was The Moon.

"Ah," the woman said. "Not so bad. Would you like the interpretation?" she asked, looking at Lucy.

Lucy nodded.

"Big change," the woman said, pointing at Death, "from old love to a new." The psychic's index finger moved from The Fool to the High Priestess. The finger hovered above The Ten of Swords. "Betrayal," the psychic said. "A secret will be revealed," she said, pointing to The Moon. Then back to The Empress. "The birth of a child."

Lucy laughed. There was nothing to this. It was all a joke.

Kay thanked the woman and paid her.

"What did you think?" Kay asked on the way back to the car.

"It was interesting, I suppose. But what a bunch of nonsense!"

"What makes you say that?"

"That corny accent, for starters."

Kay laughed. "You wanted the full experience, didn't you?"

"The birth of a child? Not likely. I had to have my ovaries removed after Hannah was born." She had a disturbing thought. If a child were coming, it would only be through Hannah. It would be tragic if Hannah got pregnant and had to give up her dreams. Lucy looked forward to having a grandchild someday, but not anytime soon. No, it was all nonsense. "Big change." Lucy laughed. "Everyone has big changes. Old love, new love." That was for soap operas. "Betrayal?" Lucy couldn't imagine! She looked at Kay as they walked. "We both got the death card."

"The death card usually doesn't mean physical death. It can be good. It always means change. The death of a lifestyle, maybe, or a bad habit. A relationship sometimes. It means different things in the context of the other cards. But in my case, it does mean physical death."

"Oh?"

"Frank has pancreatic cancer. It's terminal. He's doing a trial for a new treatment. That's why we moved to Ann Arbor. They're doing the research here."

"I'm so sorry." That was hard to hear.

"He's got six months to a year, if the treatment doesn't work. If it does, he could live to be a hundred. Whatever happens, we're going to make the best of it."

Lucy was silent for a while. Poor Frank. Poor Kay. It was too sad to think about.

"A secret will be revealed," Kay said, smirking. "I wonder what that's all about?"

"Probably nothing. It's all a bunch of hooey."

"Says you," Kay said. "We'll see."

Chapter 25

FITNESS

Lucy had never met anyone like Kay.

Kay liked to try new things. She spent an appropriate amount of time caring for Frank and their home, but she made it clear that she wasn't a slave to anyone or anything, a man or a house. She always allowed time to relax or have fun.

One day, they were sunning by the pool, and Kay said, "What do you think about running?"

Lucy said, "Running's great. I used to run in high school."

"I did a marathon once," Kay said.

That evening they went shopping for shoes, running shorts and sports tops. Kay, or rather Frank, paid for it all with the new credit card.

They met on the sidewalk at 8 am in front of their homes the next day.

Kay held her hands up to give Lucy a double high-five. "Yay! Running buddies!"

"We should walk a couple of blocks to warm up," said Lucy.

"Yeah, it's been a while. We should start slow."

After two blocks, they picked up the pace. It was already getting hot.

"Ugh," said Lucy. "I'm sweating."

"Ladies don't sweat. We glow."

"Well, I'm glowing like a pig."

After a few more blocks, Lucy slowed to a walk. "I remember why I quit running. It sucks."

"It's not for everybody," Kay said.

"Ever see anyone running with a smile on their face?"

"Come to think of it, no."

"There's a reason for that. Anyway, I think I'm more of a swimmer."

"I'm with you," Kay said. "Soak up the sun, do a couple of laps, and drink some wine. That's healthy, right?"

"Yeah, because of the antioxidants."

"Back to the pool?"

"Back to the pool."

Chapter 26

FINDING THE ZEN

Saturday, they were sunbathing at their usual time when Lucy had an idea.

"Do you feel like checking out the Zen Temple?" she asked. "It's only a few blocks away."

"Sure. I respect the wisdom of all cultures. I've always been Zen curious."

"Me, too."

"Day and time?"

Lucy picked up her phone and found the website. "Tomorrow, ten a.m."

"That's a little early for a Sunday."

"Please?"

"Okay, what the hell."

The following day, Lucy rang Kay's doorbell at 9:45. She had two travel mugs of coffee in her hands.

Kay appeared, dressed in yoga pants and a spaghetti-strap top.

Lucy handed Kay a mug.

"Thanks, sweetie."

They were met at the temple's door by a tall woman in gray robes that looked like pajamas. She had short-cropped hair and a peaceful smile.

"Welcome," she said softly. "First time?" Lucy and Kay nodded. "Please remove your shoes by the door and join everyone in the next room."

They did as instructed. In the next room were about forty men and women, most sitting on floor cushions, a few in chairs. All were meditating quietly. Lucy and Kay found two pillows beside each other and sat in the half-lotus posture like the others.

After about ten minutes, a bell rang. They opened their eyes. On a platform in the front of the room was a woman in her seventies, also dressed in gray.

"We will now chant the three refuges, first in Sino-Korean, as is our tradition."

Everyone stood and placed their hands together in front of their chests. Kay and Lucy tried to follow along as everyone chanted, but the words were meaningless to Lucy.

"Now in English," the lady priest said.

"I go for refuge to the Buddha, my deeply awakened mind, which must be cultivated to be known fully.

"I go for refuge to the Dharma, truth manifesting everywhere, which must be cultivated to be known fully.

"I go for refuge to the Sangha, deep interconnection with all beings, which must be cultivated to be known fully."

Everyone sat and meditated again. After a few minutes, the bell rang again, and the priest gave a dharma talk on the eightfold path— Buddhism in a nutshell. Suffering could be avoided if the follower could cultivate these practices.

When the dharma talk was over, it was time for questions. Kay's hand went up.

"Is pleasure bad?" she asked.

"There are reasons we feel desire and pleasure," the lady priest answered. "They are neither good nor bad by themselves. The suffering comes when we desire things we can't have or become attached to pleasure."

Kay was satisfied with the answer. "I'll have to work on that one," she told Lucy. That drew snickers from the people nearby.

On the walk home, Lucy asked, "What did you think?"

"I liked the part about non-attachment. That's what nonmonogamy's all about. Love without clinging. But honestly, I do mindfulness and meditation all the time."

"You do?"

"Yeah. What do you think I'm doing when I'm sunbathing? I Clear my mind and become one with the universe. Om."

Lucy could see her point. "But what did you think about the rest?"

"I don't know. I loved the dharma talk. I was hoping for some cute guys."

"So much for attachment to pleasure."

"Like I said, I'll have to work on that."

Chapter 27
KAY SEZ

Lucy admired Kay so much that she began taking note of the wise, funny, or peculiar things that Kay said, then she'd write them down later.

Such as: "Physical pleasure may not be the most important thing in life, but it is important. There's no reason on God's green Earth to deny yourself."

And: "Love means never having to say you're sorry? Give me a break. If you love somebody, you're going to hurt them sometimes. If you don't apologize, that just makes you an asshole."

And: "Life is good when the people you love can love each other."

And: "Pain is mandatory; suffering is optional."

Lucy asked her what she meant when she said that one.

"We think of pain and suffering as the same thing," Kay said, "but there's a difference. Pain's a neurological response to something that's unhealthy for the organism. Every creature experiences pain. It evolved to keep us alive. But suffering's a psychological reaction to something that might not even be real."

"That's deep," Lucy said.

"Oh, I didn't come up with that—that was the lady priest at the Zen temple."

"I don't remember her saying that."

"Because you fell asleep during the second round of meditation," Kay said. She smacked Lucy on the back of the head. "Stay awake every moment!" she said.

Chapter 28

GIRLS' NIGHT OUT

The new fitness routine consisted of sunning, fifteen minutes on each side while drinking wine, two laps in the pool, and more sunning and wine. And repeat.

One day they were by the pool. Lucy was doing a crossword puzzle.

"'Non-physical entity arising from a group consciousness…'" Lucy said. "Eight letters. Begins and ends with the letter 'e.'"

Kay thought for a second."Oh! Egregore."

"I've never heard that one. How do you spell it?"

"E-g-r-e-g-o-r-e."

"Wow. It fits."

Kay said, "I'm bored."

"What do you feel like doing?" Lucy was content but up for anything Kay wanted to do.

"I feel like going out. This burg has to have a dance club, right?"

"I think so."

"Wanna go tonight?"

"Don't you think we're a little old for that sort of thing?"

"Nonsense. Are we beautiful?"

"Yes, we are."

"Are we hot?"

"Absolutely."

"I'm a sexy love goddess, and you're my goddess-in-training. It would be a shame to deprive the world of all this divine beauty and hotness."

Lucy laughed. "Okay."

"We'll make all the young girls jealous."

Naturally, they had to go shopping for suitable dresses. Kay bought Lucy a dark blue minidress that was too revealing for Lucy's comfort--too much cleavage, too much leg. But Kay was paying for it, so Lucy let her have her way. Kay bought one for herself, made of a deep green stretchy fabric, figure-hugging and even more revealing than Lucy's.

When she got home, Alex was in his basement office. She made sure he had something to eat, and she got dressed. She put more effort into her makeup than she had in a long time.

She went downstairs to say goodbye to Alex.

"What do you think?" she asked.

He looked up from his computer. "Wow..." he said.

"You don't think it's too much? Or too little?"

"You look amazing. It's high time you got out and had some fun. I think Kay is a good influence on you."

Alex had desire in his eyes, and she basked in it. He wanted to embrace her and struggled to rise from the chair. She spared him the effort by going to him. She gave him a warm kiss.

"If you don't stay out too late, I'll help you get out of that sexy little dress," he said.

"Fat chance. You'll be asleep by ten. I might not get home until you leave for work."

He laughed. “Have a good time, but be careful. You and Kay stick together. And don’t leave your drinks unattended.”

“Yes, Daddy. I’ll be careful.”

He laughed again.

The line outside the club wasn’t long and moved quickly. The music from inside made the brick wall vibrate.

“That dress was made for you,” Kay said.

“Thanks for buying it.”

“Thank Frank next time you see him. It really shows off your figure. I wish I had boobs like that.”

“Your boobs are fine.”

“They’re okay. I’m trying to talk Frank into buying me a new pair.”

Lucy laughed as she showed her ID at the door.

Inside, she wondered for a second if they’d made a mistake. The music was loud, and the patrons were young.

But in this light, Kay could pass for twenty-five. That meant that Lucy could pass, too.

“Let’s find a table,” Kay said. They plunged in.

They started getting attention right away. There were younger women, but none more attractive than they were, at least in the dim light of the club.

Kay found an empty table. A waitress brought drinks to them as soon as they sat.

“That was quick,” Kay said, looking around for the man who bought them. An attractive man at the bar with graying temples and a suit raised his glass. Kay acknowledged him with a nod and a smile.

"What do you think this is?" Lucy said, looking at the cocktail in front of her.

Kay took a sip. "Mimosa," she said.

"Hmm. Tasty."

"If we work this right, we can drink for free all night."

"I don't know. It feels kind of dishonest."

"A drink is a gift, not a commitment. When a man buys a drink for a woman, it's like playing the lottery. He doesn't expect to hit the jackpot every time."

"What happens if you meet somebody you'd like to hook up with?"

"Don't worry. You're my date for the evening. But I do feel like flirting."

"That's fine," Lucy said. "I feel like flirting, too. But it's been a while. I wouldn't know where to start."

"It's easy. Summon your inner goddess." Lucy gave Kay an amused glance. "Everyone has a little bit of The Goddess in them," Kay said, "even men. Most people ignore her, and she goes away. If you acknowledge her, she gives your life power and joy. She keeps you young."

"How do I do that?"

"Talk to her. Invite her in."

"Out loud?" Lucy asked.

Kay laughed. "No, not here. We're trying to attract men, not scare them off. Silently ask her to join you. Offer your body as a vessel."

Lucy was quiet for a moment. "Okay. What now?"

"Now energize your, um, *pneumatiki dynami*. Spirit energy. Charisma, animal magnetism, charm. They're all different flavors of the same ice cream."

"That's a little weird."

"Try it. Visualize a blue light around your body." Lucy closed her eyes to concentrate. "Keep your eyes open, sweetie," Kay said, "or the waitress will cut us off."

Lucy smiled. This was strange but fun. "I feel all tingly. Sexy."

"Good. Now you're ready to flirt. Have you picked out a victim, er, target?"

Lucy nodded in the direction of a handsome young man three tables away. He wasn't looking their way.

"Alright," Kay said. "Now focus your aura. Imagine it reaching out to him like a blue mist. Reach out and—I don't know— stroke his cheek or something."

Lucy imagined a soft blue mist. It floated gently from her until it reached the man and caressed his face. He slowly turned their way. Lucy smiled at him, and he smiled back.

"Wow," Lucy said.

"Great! You're a natural," Kay said.

It was incredible.

It felt like the first time she saw Alex. And that reminded Lucy she was married.

"Okay," she said. "That's enough." She didn't want to take this thing too far.

They finished their drinks and made their way to the dance floor. Lucy didn't care for the music but loved to move her body this way. They danced with each other and sometimes random men for a while, without expectations or pressure.

There was a break in the music, and they returned to their table. The man with the graying temples was looking their way.

"He's going to ask to sit with us," Kay said. "Is that okay?"

"I suppose."

"If he focuses on you, and you don't want the attention, just display your wedding ring. Simple."

"What if he focuses on you?"

"I'll give him my number if he's worthy."

As Kay predicted, the man approached and asked if he could sit with them. Kay gave him permission, and he ordered another round of drinks. They introduced themselves and made small talk. He made sure that they knew he was a lawyer with his own practice. Using her left hand, Lucy played with her mimosa to make sure he saw her wedding ring. He turned his attention to Kay and began telling her about his work. The music started again, and Kay got to her feet.

"Come on, girlfriend! Time to burn off those mimosas."

The man followed them onto the dance floor, where they danced in a group of three. The man whispered something to Kay. She stroked his arm and shook her head. He nodded politely and moved on to dance with another woman.

"Did he ask for your number?" Lucy asked.

"Yeah. I didn't give it to him. I don't mind lawyers, but I don't want to talk about the job. He was putting me to sleep. The night is still young."

The music ended again, and they headed back to their table. Lucy cried out, stopped in her tracks, and turned.

"What?" Kay asked.

"Someone just grabbed my ass."

Kay laughed. "Did you enjoy it?"

"No! I feel violated!"

Kay frowned and looked for the culprit. A man in a hockey jersey, with friends on each side, was laughing hysterically. He gave his friends a high five.

"Who did it?" Kay yelled.

The men on either side pointed to their friend in the middle.

Kay calmly walked up to him.

"What are you gonna do about it?" the cretin asked.

He continued to laugh until he saw the look in her eyes.

"You're not worthy!" she hissed. She grabbed his jersey at the shoulders before he could escape and kneed him hard in the groin. He fell to the floor, coughing and moaning. His friends were both surprised and amused. They picked him up and helped him to the door.

Lucy expected to be thrown out of the club, but few people saw the incident.

Their waitress brought over another round of drinks.

"These are on me," she said. "For taking care of the creep. Thanks."

"My hero," Lucy said, raising her glass.

When Lucy got home at 2 in the morning, she went to the spare room to check on Alex. He was asleep, of course. It was a shame because she was feeling frisky.

She had to get out of that sexy little dress all by herself.

Chapter 29
AU NATUREL

Lucy met Kay by the pool one day for sunbathing. She had two bottles of wine ready in a cooler filled with ice.

"What a beautiful day," Kay said. She spread a towel on her lounge chair and took off her bikini.

"What are you doing?" Lucy asked.

"Getting a good tan without the lines," Kay said. She was so bold. "When I was growing up, we didn't wear a lot of clothes. I've never totally gotten used to them. Try it. You might like it." She took a drink of wine. Lucy hesitated. "Frank's golfing. He won't be back until dinner. We've got a nice privacy fence. No one can see."

So Lucy removed her bikini, too. "I wouldn't want you to think I'm a prude."

"Heavens, no. Doesn't it feel good? There's nothing as liberating as being naked under the sun."

They basked for a while. Kay said, "Time for a dip."

She got to her feet and dove into the water. Lucy followed. It was pleasant, with nothing between her skin and the world. She felt every ripple, every bubble. Every cell in her body woke up and came alive.

She swam to the far end of the pool, then swam deep on the return.

When she surfaced, a muscular young man in trunks was dipping a net into the pool.

"Yike!" she said. She flailed, submerged, surfaced, and tried to regain her composure.

"Hi, Eric," Kay said.

"Mrs. Holloway," the young man said.

"I'd like you to meet my friend Lucy. She lives next door. Lucy, this is Eric from the pool service."

"Kay, I'm naked."

"Lucy, where are your manners?" Kay laughed, tickled by Lucy's embarrassment. "Eric, Lucy's shy. Could you turn around while we get her covered up?"

"Sure thing, Mrs. Holloway." He turned around.

Lucy was flustered and angry as she climbed out of the pool. She wrapped the towel around her and picked up her bikini from the patio.

"Isn't he the best thing you've seen all day?" Kay whispered.

"I suppose." Lucy looked at Eric. "Yes, he's very attractive."

"And your face is an attractive shade of red," Kay said.

"I have to go."

"See you tomorrow?"

"We'll see."

Lucy took a shower to rinse off the chlorine. By the time she was dry, she wasn't angry anymore.

Kay was Kay. It was hard to stay mad at her.

Chapter 30

THE BIG OH

Lucy expected Kay to be by the pool the next day at the usual time. Instead, she found Kay lugging a large futon to the back of the yard, balanced on her head. The futon almost covered her petite frame, and she couldn't see where she was going. It was comical.

"Here, let me help," Lucy said.

"Thank goodness. I thought I could do it myself."

They dropped the futon under the tree house at the foot of the ladder.

Kay looked up. "I don't know..."

"Maybe if we rolled it up like a burrito?"

"It's worth a shot."

They were able to fold it in half. Kay grabbed one end and started up the ladder. Lucy grabbed the other end and pushed. The futon barely fit through the trap door but with a lot of effort, they were able to get it inside.

Kay placed the futon where she wanted it and unfurled a sheet. There were candles, a cooler with bottles of wine, gauze drapes at the windows, and a portable stereo.

"Wow," said Lucy. "You're going all out."

"I told myself when I was a girl that if I ever got a treehouse, I'd make good use of it. Why let the boys have all the fun?"

Kay fluffed a pillow and dropped it on the futon. She motioned to Lucy to try it out, and Lucy lay down.

"I got the footlocker open."

"Yeah? Let's see!"

Kay held up a comic book. "January 2016 X-Men." And a magazine. "November 2019 Penthouse."

"Joey Rosetti, you naughty boy!"

Kay held up some small, square packages.

"Three Trojan condoms. Ribbed for her pleasure."

Lucy gasped. "Oh, my gosh! Do you suppose he tried to use those with Hannah?"

"If he did, at least he was playing safe. Kudos to him."

"Maybe he was pressuring her for sex. Maybe that's why they stopped spending time together."

"God forbid your daughter have any fun," Kay teased.

"She's a child."

"Where I come from, they'd have two or three kids at her age." Kay held up a bag of weed and rolling papers. "And lastly..."

"Wow, I had Joey all wrong. He seemed so clean-cut.

"I try not to judge."

Kay sat on the futon and started rolling a joint.

"You're not going to smoke that, are you?" Lucy asked.

"I sure am. When was the last time you got high?"

"College."

Kay lit the joint and inhaled. "Not bad. I thought it would be old and gross." She passed the joint to Lucy.

"No, I couldn't."

"It's legal here now."

"I really shouldn't."

"I hear words but no conviction."

Lucy slowly reached for the joint. She smiled impishly.

"That's my girl." Lucy took a drag. "You have to inhale." Lucy tried it again, deeper this time. She coughed.

Kay got to her feet and returned to the futon with a wine bottle and two glasses. She sat and poured the wine. She handed a glass to Lucy and raised the other in a toast.

"To us," she said.

"To us." She and Lucy drank.

Kay took the Penthouse magazine off the floor and thumbed through it. Lucy looked on.

"They're pretty," Lucy said.

"Yeah, but who knows what they're like under the big boobs and flawless skin? Can they make conversation? Can they do basic math? Are they nice people?"

"Maybe you're jealous?"

"I don't get jealous. But I wouldn't mind being that well-endowed."

"You're beautiful," Lucy said. "And special. I've never met anyone like you."

"That's because there isn't anyone like me," said Kay.

They finished the joint and looked through the magazine, skipping the articles and looking at the pictures. Lucy was fascinated. She had never seen a so-called men's magazine.

When Lucy was done looking, she laid it on the floor. She saw a faint blue light in the corner of her eye. She looked at Kay, who was staring into space, deep in thought.

"You have to break some eggs to make a good quiche," Kay said.

Lucy laughed. "What's that supposed to mean?"

"Nothing. I just like a good quiche."

"Are you stoned?"

"Maybe a little," Kay said. "How about you?"

"Yeah. This was a good idea. I feel so relaxed!"

Kay put on music and lit some candles.

Lucy looked around the tree house.

"You've done a good job fixing this place up," she said. "It's almost...r omantic."

"I try."

Kay returned to the futon. She lay facing Lucy, their bodies touching.

"What's that scent?" Lucy asked.

"Cinnamon and sandalwood."

"Very nice."

Lucy felt an emotion that she couldn't identify. She closed her eyes. Kay kissed her on the forehead like Alex often did. Lucy snuggled in closer to Kay. Kay's hand stroked Lucy's side from her arm down to her waist. It was nice to be touched that way. Alex didn't do that often. She sighed. Kay put a hand under Lucy's shirt and stroked the same way, but with fingers on skin now. It gave Lucy goosebumps. She giggled. She wondered where this was going.

Kay's fingers came around to the front and stroked Lucy's belly. Lucy snorted.

"That tickles," she said.

"Would you like me to stop?" Kay asked.

"No, continue."

Kay's hand slowly made its way down until her fingers slid into the waistband of Lucy's shorts.

Lucy had a giggle fit.

"What are you doing?" Lucy asked. Kay cupped her face and stopped her giggles with a kiss. It was unexpected. It was wonderful. It made Lucy dizzy.

Kay backed off and looked into Lucy's eyes. "Would you like me to stop?"

"No, continue," Lucy whispered. The words just came out. Lucy had lost control. Her heart was pounding.

Kay kissed her again, harder this time. Her fingers probed deeper into Lucy's shorts. She kissed across Lucy's cheek to the earlobe and licked.

"Oh!" Lucy said. Her fingers, all on their own, undid the buttons of Kay's shirt and opened it to expose Kay's breasts.

They kissed. They helped each other shed their clothing. They made love with their fingers, their lips, and their tongues. Kay brought Lucy to the edge of consciousness. Lucy felt her legs and ass tighten and relax involuntarily, in waves, again and again. It felt like the ocean crashing inside her, each wave getting more intense, over and over. She heard herself moaning as she got closer to the edge. She was afraid someone else would hear.

She put a hand over her mouth to muffle the sounds.

When the biggest wave came, it crashed over her whole being.

As she came, she cried, "Eep!"

Chapter 31
AFTERGLOW

When Lucy woke, the weed and wine were wearing off. Their bodies were entangled, with Kay's head nestled in the crook of Lucy's neck. Lucy's arm had gone numb. She pulled it away to get the feeling back. That woke Kay.

"What in the world just happened?" Lucy asked.

"You had a really good orgasm, I think."

"Yeah. Now I see what all the fuss is about."

"You've never had one before?"

"Not like that!"

"I forgot to mention—I like women, too."

"No kidding." That made two of them, evidently. Surprise! Her brows furrowed. "Oh, Jesus."

"Is there a problem?" Kay asked.

"Well, yeah! We just had sex! I have a husband!"

"So do I. It's really not that big of a deal."

"For you! You had it all worked out before you got married!" Lucy covered her eyes and groaned. "I have to tell Alex, don't I?"

"Yeah. This won't work unless everyone's honest with each other."

"What do I say? He'll be hurt."

"Maybe for a while. But the truth always hurts less in the long run."

"How could I not know? I feel so stupid!"

"Don't beat yourself up. The culture's brainwashed everyone."

"You knew."

"I told you, I can read people. I'm never wrong." Kay hugged her. "You're going to be ok."

"I've got to go. I've got some thinking to do."

That was an understatement.

She got dressed and went down the ladder.

"Call me later!" Kay said.

When Lucy got home, her skin was damp from making love. She didn't shower right away. She could still smell Kay on her skin.

She spent the afternoon thinking.

She had never had that intense experience with Alex. Her climax reminded her of giving birth to Hannah, the way her body had contracted and relaxed, the way everything had built up to the end. Only this time, the intense pain had been replaced by intense pleasure.

What had she given birth to this time? A new life. A new Lucy. A new set of problems she would have to deal with sooner or later.

She thought about the Tarot reading—big change, from old love to new. A secret will be revealed. Betrayal. It had all come true in one fell swoop.

She remembered her friend Taylor. The summer she met Alex, they had spent a lot of time together, at Taylor's family cabin up north. Swimming, drinking, and flirting with boys that never had a chance. They'd had a lot of fun together. They had a deep affection for each other and had made out of few times, just playing around. One night after Lollapalooza, Taylor got really drunk and kissed Lucy in a way that wasn't just innocent fun. It wasn't just playing around that time. Taylor had wanted more than Lucy could give her then.

Oh, poor Taylor!

The next time she saw Hannah, Lucy said, "Your old boyfriend had us all fooled, didn't he? Everybody thought he was such a straight arrow."

"What do you mean?"

She told Hannah what Kay had found in Joey's old footlocker. Hannah confirmed that the comic book was Joey's—he'd had a large collection of them.

Then Hannah made a confession—the condoms were hers. Lucy was stunned, then relieved. They'd raised a smart daughter. She knew how to protect herself. She wouldn't be getting pregnant until she was ready. The psychic had been wrong about that, anyway.

The marijuana was something else altogether.

"It's not Joey's," Hannah said. "He's straight-edge."

"What does that mean?"

"He doesn't do drugs or alcohol. He won't even take Tylenol for a headache."

"Are you sure about that?"

"Positive. And he had to pass a drug test to get into the Naval Academy. He wasn't going to take any chances."

That confirmed Lucy's suspicions. The whole thing had been a set-up.

It was obvious what had happened. Kay had purposefully seduced her. The scented candles, the futon. The wine, the weed, the Penthouse magazine to awaken that part of her. Kay had set the stage for seduction. It hadn't been spontaneous at all. It had all been carefully thought out.

It didn't matter. It was what she had needed, and Kay had known somehow.

Lucy decided she had to continue seeing Kay.

She also decided to tell Alex everything, whatever the consequences.

She just never got around to actually doing it.

Chapter 32

BACK IN THE GROOVE

Lucy saw Kay every day. They made love frequently, sometimes in the treehouse, sometimes in Lucy's bed, and once, in a passionate fever, by Kay's pool in the afternoon.

Lucy got the urge to create again. She had loved to draw and paint in school but had given it up after getting her art degree, ironically. She had become a wife and a mother, so she had other priorities. Being a homemaker became her art. Alex had never demanded that of her and was surprised she had lost interest. He had never pressured her one way or the other.

Now, though: Alex was low-maintenance, Hannah was on auto-pilot, and this new thing with Kay didn't take up much of her time. This was the time that Lucy had been waiting for, a time for self-expression.

She went to the attic and looked for her old art supplies. She found an easel and some sketch pads. She found the large storage bin that contained her oil paints and brushes, but the paint had all dried. It had been over twenty years.

She found a plastic bag with a dozen or so charcoals. It was good enough. She would start there.

She took the easel, the sketch pad, and the charcoals to the patio. It was a pleasant day and a good setting for being creative. She began to sketch and found that it came right back to her after all these years. The drawing took shape—her muse Kay, drawn from memory. Kay was nude, her left leg bent and splayed to the side, right knee up, with both hands on it. She looked straight ahead with a smile that was sexy, impish, almost defiant. When Lucy saw Kay in her mind, she looked like this.

When Alex got home from work, he saw the easel on the patio and smiled. "You're painting again," he said.

"Drawing, for now."

He opened the doors to the patio and looked at the sketch."It's Kay," he said. "Wow. It's beautiful."

"*She's* beautiful," Lucy said. "She's my inspiration."

She chose those words carefully. She hoped Alex would read between the lines and see that her relationship with Kay was more than a friendship. Maybe it would soften the blow for the time to come when she would have to be blunt and cruel and tell him the whole truth. But he didn't pick up on it.

"Did you get her to pose for you?"

"No, I did it from memory."

She hoped he'd ask, "When did you see her nude like this?"

She'd reply, "We see each other nude all the time."

Then he'd ask why, and she'd say because they were lovers.

None of that happened. He admired the sketch for a while, then said, "Keep up the good work." He went to his office in the basement.

The poor, dear man remained clueless.

Lucy felt like a coward.

Chapter 33

OPERATION II

Lucy packed Alex's overnight bag the night before the surgery. She was as anxious as he was. She tried to stay calm. Freaking out wouldn't do any good.

Morning came. She woke her husband and helped him get into a t-shirt and sweatpants.

When he reached the front door, he tried to pick up the overnight bag Lucy had put there.

"I've got that, baby," she said.

"Okay," he said. "Where's my laptop?"

"You won't need it. You'll be unconscious the whole time."

She opened the front door for him. He hobbled to the driver's side of the car out of habit.

"No, sweetie, I'm driving," she said.

"Okay."

He headed for the other side of the car.

At the hospital, Lucy helped him into a wheelchair. He was taken to his room, and Lucy helped him change into a hospital gown. He was in pain, and she felt it with him. She couldn't wait for it to be over.

"Would you like to watch tv ?" Lucy asked. "It might get your mind off things."

"Yes."

She picked up the remote and turned on the tv. On the screen, a fit young man hawked exercise equipment on an infomercial.

"What would you like to watch?"

"Doesn't matter. That's fine." Alex said.

The anesthetist hooked up a machine to his IV.

"How's the pain, Mr. Herman? On a scale of one to ten?"

"Twelve," he said. His face twisted in agony.

"It's going to be a few more hours, but we'll make you comfortable." She ran a line from a machine into a port on his IV tube. She handed him a control pendant and pointed. "When you need some relief, press this button."

Alex pressed the button right away, and the machine beeped. He waited a while, then hit the button again. The machine beeped again.

Lucy kissed him on the forehead. "I'll see you when you wake up. Love you, baby."

He looked at her. His eyes were glassy.

"Love you, too," he slurred. He hit the button again, three times.

Lucy was alarmed.

"Is that safe?" she asked the anesthetist.

"He can't overdose, but it lets him feel like he has some control."

·♥·♥·♥·♥·♥·

Lucy called Kay on the walk back to the car.

"I've got Alex all settled in."

"How's he doing?"

"Out cold by now."

"Frank and I are buying flowers and a get-well card. What room is he in?"

"He'll be home tomorrow night. Just bring them over to the house."

"Okay." There was a pause. "Have you told him yet?"

"No. There's never a good time."

"There never *will* be a good time. I told Frank last night."

"What did he say?"

"He says we're cute together."

"Just make sure he doesn't spill the beans, okay? I have to be the one."

"Frank knows better than that. But don't wait too long."

"I won't."

"Love you, girlfriend."

"Love you, too."

Chapter 34

THE WAITING ROOM

Madison set the bouquet on the table beside her in the waiting room. The flowers were bright yellow, meant to be cheery and healing. The florist had added deep green ferns for contrast. The card said the bouquet was from the staff of Tucker-Herman, but Madison had picked it out and paid for it herself. The card was meant to deflect suspicion. Alex was oblivious. Brad, being more worldly, was starting to get wise.

A pretty blond woman came in, smiled a greeting, and sat on the other side of the room. The woman was settling in when her phone buzzed. She looked at it and gave an exclamation of annoyance. She pressed the screen on the phone and held it to her ear.

"This is Lucy Herman," she said.

That got Madison's attention —this was Alex's wife, who was frowning now.

"I just got a fraud alert on my credit card," she said to Madison, the only other person there. Lucy listened for a while, nodding. "Yes, cancel the transactions and cancel the cards, please. Thank you for catching it."

She put the phone away and looked at Madison. "Can you believe it? My husband's in the hospital, and some crook just bought five thousand dollars worth of exercise equipment with our account."

"The nerve," Madison said.

"Some people!" Lucy shook her head.

A doctor walked into the waiting room. "Mrs. Herman?" he said. "Mr. Herman is out of surgery. Everything went well. He's back in his room. He'll be waking up soon."

Lucy got to her feet and followed the doctor.

Madison sat alone, thinking.

Alex's wife looked like a nice person.

Madison looked at the bouquet.

What am I doing here? she asked herself.

Hell if I know, she answered.

Chapter 35
IN ANESTHESIA VERITAS

Lucy sat in the chair next to Alex's bed. She saw his phone, wallet, and credit card on the tray table. She connected the logical dots. She put the card in the wallet and put the wallet in her purse.

She held his hand and looked at his serene expression. He made some interesting noises waking up, but it took a half-hour before he could talk. He finally sighed and looked around.

"Lucy," he said.

"Hi, sweetie. How do you feel?"

"Good," he said slowly. He reached out to the tray table and felt around. "My wallet," he said.

"I've got it."

"Okay."

"Have you been buying things?" she asked.

"Yeah."

"Exercise equipment?"

"Yeah."

"Why?"

"So I can get buff and handsome. So you'll love me again."

It stung. Her eyes teared up. The anesthesia freed him to say what he really felt. It was unusual for him.

She caressed his cheek. "Oh, sweetie. I *do* love you. I love you more than anything."

And it was true.

Chapter 36

KAY SERA, SERA

The surgery was successful. Alex came home and was on the mend.

After their next rendezvous in the tree house, Kay told Lucy, "I've got a date tomorrow night."

The words wounded Lucy. "With who?" she asked. "The pool boy?"

"With *whom.* No. Someone at the country club needs me."

Lucy was hurt but tried not to show it. The old Lucy, depressed Lucy, would have been crushed.

Lucy was silent for a while. "But I need you," she said. "I love you."

"I love you, too. And you love Alex, and I love Frank. I'm sorry, but I love humanity—the whole species. What you're feeling right now isn't love. It's jealousy. You'll have to get over it."

"I believe in monogamy," Lucy said.

"I do, too. But not for me. Do you really love me?"

"Yes."

"Just the way I am?"

"Absolutely."

"Then don't try to change me." Kay kissed her. "You'll be okay. I promise."

Chapter 37

PICNIC II

Alex had recovered enough to lug a full cooler from the kitchen to the entryway. He set it next to the front door.

"Are you sure you don't want to come?" he called out.

"I'm not going out in this heat for one of Brad's social events. Kay and I are going to hang out by the pool."

"It'll be just as hot there."

"But arm's length from clean water and air conditioning."

"Come on by if you change your mind."

"Will do. Have a good time. Don't forget the sunscreen!" she said as he closed the front door.

Kay was on a lounge chair by the pool, wearing only sunglasses. Lucy kissed her.

"Where's Frank?" Lucy asked.

"Golfing, of course. He won't be back until dinner."

"Okay, then." Lucy stripped off her clothes and lay on the lounge chair beside Kay's.

They sunbathed briefly. Kay said, "I'm bored."

"What do you feel like doing?"

"I don't know. Any ideas?"

"We could crash Alex's company picnic."

"I'm surprised you didn't say something before now."

"I didn't think you'd be interested." She had wanted to keep Kay to herself today.

They got dressed and drove to the park.

Lucy saw Brad at the picnic shelter he always reserved for the annual event.

"You'll like Brad," Lucy said as they approached. "He's handsome and rich."

"He does sound like my type."

"Brad!" Lucy said. She hugged him. "This is my friend Kay."

"Nice to meet you," Kay said.

"Alex said you had other plans," Brad said.

"Changed my mind."

"Oh, look!" Kay said. "Frisbee!" She trotted off to play frisbee with Bob and Garth.

Lucy spotted Alex and a woman in a pedal boat. The woman looked familiar. The two looked like they were enjoying each other's company. Lucy frowned.

"Who's that with Alex?" she asked.

"Madison Lundquist. She's helping out with sales."

"They seem to be having a good time. Should I be worried?"

"You know Alex isn't that kind of guy."

She waved dismissively. "I know. I'm being silly."

"I could introduce you—put your mind at ease."

"Actually, I think we've met. I just stopped by to say hi. We've got things to do. Do me a favor— don't tell Alex I was here."

"Is everything alright?"

"Of course. Kay!" she called out. Kay trotted back to Lucy's side.

They walked along the river back to the car.

"Why are we leaving so soon?" Kay asked.

Lucy pointed at Alex and Madison.

"Is that Alex?"

"Yeah."

It had been a long time since Lucy had seen Alex act like that. He looked...happy.

"Who's that with him?"

"Madison Lundquist," Lucy said mockingly. "Sales."

"Wow. You're jealous." Kay looked amused.

"Am not."

Kay gasped.

"Do you think they're having an affair?" asked Kay, pretending to be outraged.

"Don't be ridiculous."

"That son of a bitch!" Kay teased. "Cheating on my best friend!"

"Stop. You've made your point."

"I say we get even."

"And how would we do that?" She looked at Kay, already sorry she'd asked.

"Let's go to your house and fuck."

Lucy pushed Kay on the shoulder, almost knocking her over.

"I think you're too wild for me," Lucy said.

"Oh, I've heard *that* before," Kay replied.

But they did go to Lucy's and fuck. Not for revenge, but "just because."

Chapter 38

JULY 24TH

Alex had a good memory for special dates. Lucy, not so much. She always remembered the big ones—birthdays, christenings, weddings with their associated anniversaries, et cetera. But she had a problem with the more nebulous dates—the anniversary of the first time she ever saw her husband, for instance.

On the morning of July 24th, she and Alex had breakfast together. He got dressed, kissed her goodbye, and went to work.

She did some housework and a crossword puzzle. At one in the afternoon, she met Kay by the pool for sunbathing and wine. By two pm, Kay had talked her into a massage.

They showered together in Lucy's master bath and began making love. They dried each other off. By the time they got into bed, thoughts of a conventional massage were forgotten.

Kay was on top. She kissed Lucy.

"I smell flowers," Lucy said.

"I smell vanilla," said Kay, and she kissed Lucy on the neck.

"That's my body wash."

"Mmm," said Kay.

Kay was an expert at this, having both experience and passion. She took her time. Kay kissed her way down to Lucy's breasts while Lucy stroked her hair.

"Kori tis Thalassis," Lucy said. Kay looked at her and smiled. "I like saying your name," Lucy said.

"I like hearing you say it," Kay said. "Lucy...Lucia della mia vita. Light of my life."

"Kori tis Thalassis...Kori tis Thalassis...Kori tis Thalassis..." Lucy whispered as if it were an incantation.

Kay kissed and licked down Lucy's body. She worked slowly. Lucy thought she would die from anticipation before Kay's tongue reached her clitoris.

"Kori tis Thalassis...Kori tis Thalassis...Oh...my...God!" Lucy moaned. She convulsed and came.

Wow! Best orgasm ever!

Madison passed Alex's office on the way to the break room.

That's odd.

She backed up and knocked on the door. She could see he was there, but he didn't answer. She opened the door and went in.

"I thought you were gone for the day," she said.

"I thought so, too," he said. He didn't look well. He reminded her of those photographs she'd seen of British soldiers evacuated from Dunkirk. He looked shell-shocked.

"Are you okay?"

"I don't know."

That worried her.

"Should I call an ambulance?"

"No. I'm fine. Really."

She wasn't convinced.

"Are you coming to the bar tonight?" she asked, to end the awkward silence.

"I don't know what I'm going to do."

The statement was broad. It could have referred to the bar or his future. There was sadness in his voice.

She noticed the bouquet on his desk. "Nice flowers. Let me put them in some water for you." She picked them up.

"Oh, the asters," he said. "Thanks."

Madison left.

Chapter 39
OLÉ!

The Grotto was the favorite watering hole of the Tucker-Herman staff. The drinks there were reasonably priced and generous, the waitstaff was friendly, and it hosted the best trivia night in town, earning everyone's loyalty.

Brad bought the first round, as he had promised. When those drinks were gone, he went to the bar to make the acquaintance of an attractive woman who looked as though she might be a flight attendant.

Tucker-Herman occupied two tables in the corner. Madison sat where she could see people coming in. Lilith was on her right, and Garth was on her left.

"Look who's here," said Garth.

Madison looked up to see Alex at the entrance. He had put his blazer on. She waved and called to him.

"That's odd," said Bob. "He never hangs out on Friday night."

Alex headed their way.

"What's everyone drinking?" He signaled the waitress. "Next round's on me. Whatever they're having. And a round of shots. Tequila?"

That got everyone's approval.

Garth stood and offered Alex his seat, allowing him to sit next to Madison.

"Glad you could make it," Madison said.

"Yeah, well, I need to get out more. How's everyone's work going?"

Lilith said, "Hey, no talking shop."

"Fair enough."

The waitress set a tray of tequila shots in the middle of the table. Alex took one and downed it. "Opa!" he said.

"That's for Ouzo," said Bob.

"What do you say for tequila?"

"I don't know. Olé, maybe?"

Alex took another shot glass. "I'll just practice until I get it right." He swallowed the shot. "Olé!" he said. Everyone applauded.

Madison excused herself to go to the ladies' room. She stopped to talk to Brad.

"Something's wrong with Alex," she said.

Brad looked at Alex and frowned. "What's he doing here?"

"I don't know, but he's doing tequila shots."

Brad looked worried. "That's not good. He doesn't drink."

"He does now, and he's really knockin' 'em down."

"Keep an eye on him for me."

"Will do, boss."

Alex matched everyone drink for drink, shot for shot. He had no tolerance for alcohol. He got trashed quickly.

He pulled a permanent marker from the inside pocket of his blazer and drew a face on his right hand—eyes with long lashes and full, sensual lips.

"What are you doing?" Madison asked.

He shredded a cocktail napkin, turning it into a wig that he placed on top of his hand.

"Hey, big boy..." the hand said in a comical falsetto. "Buy a girl a drink?"

Everyone roared with laughter.

"Go away," Alex said to the hand puppet. "You look like trouble."

"Wow!" Garth said. "You're really drunk!"

"So drunk..." Alex agreed.

The hand puppet nibbled at his ear.

"Stop it! I'm married!"

Everyone roared.

The comic in Alex's mind eventually ran out of material. He quietly sipped tequila. The hand puppet pretended to drink along with him.

He yawned. He looked at his watch.

"Oh, my," he said. "Way past my bedtime. I've enjoyed spending time with you fine people. We should do this more often." He stood up, lost his balance, and had to sit again.

"It's not even midnight," Garth said.

"Let me call you an Uber," said Madison.

"I'm fine," he said as he headed for the door.

Madison followed him.

In the parking lot, he paused and wobbled, trying to remember where he'd parked his car.

"You can't drive like this. I'll take you home." He stopped, disoriented. "Alex. This way."

"Okay."

She led him to her car. As they left the parking lot, she said, "How about some food?"

"That sounds awesome."

They went through the drive-through of a Mcdonald's. She steered the car south on State Street, out into the country, and turned onto a secluded dirt road.

"Where are we going?" he asked.

"I found a place," she said. "It's quiet, and you can really see the stars."

She stopped the car at a dead-end, surrounded by cornfields and woods. She turned the car off.

"Come on," she said.

She led him to a fallen tree trunk at the right height for sitting and star-gazing. The city was far away, so street lights didn't interfere.

"I come here sometimes when I'm sad," Madison said. They ate for a while in silence. Then Madison asked him, "When was the last time you got this drunk?"

"I've never been this drunk."

"Is something wrong?"

"Yeah."

"Wanna talk about it?"

"No."

"Trouble with the wife?"

Alex looked at her silently.

"There's a bouquet that never made it to the intended recipient. If you need to talk, I'm right here. It might help."

"Thanks. You're helping already." He sighed. "You were a psych major. Do you believe in fugues?"

"They're controversial. And rare. I've never met anyone that's had one."

"I had one today."

"Wow. They're supposed to be triggered by some kind of trauma. What happened?"

He opened his mouth and winced hard.

"I-I-I..." he stammered. "I can't even say it."

She put a hand on his back and looked into his eyes.

"I'm sorry," she said. "You can talk to me when you're ready." She looked up. "Look at those stars!"

"This is a nice spot," he said.

They finished their meals quietly.

She smacked her arm. "Mosquito," she said.

"Yep. They found us."

"Time to go," she said.

"It was nice while it lasted."

He wanted her to take him back to The Grotto to get his car, but he was still too drunk to drive. She drove him to his house.

He was hoping that Lucy would be asleep when he got home. He didn't want to deal with anything right now. But the light in the master bedroom was on.

Madison parked the car at the curb.

"Thanks for the lift," he said. "And the conversation."

"My pleasure."

The hand puppet came up and kissed Madison on the cheek.

He faked a smile and ventured forth to face whatever was coming next.

Chapter 40

CONFRONTATION

He tried to be quiet coming into the house but was still very drunk. He lost his balance removing his shoes and bumped loudly into the wall. He hesitated at the foot of the stairs. He wasn't in the mood for a confrontation.

He crept up the stairs and tried to sneak past the door of the master bedroom.

"Alex?" Lucy said.

He entered the room.

"Where have you been?"

"Having drinks with the crew. Is that ok?"

"Sure, but you should have called. I've been worried."

"Really?"

"Yes. Drinks? What's the matter with you? Are you drunk?"

"Yep. I am trashed. How was your day?"

"Good. Kay came over and gave me a massage."

"I know! I came home in time for the happy ending!"

They stared at each other for a moment. Tears gathered in her eyes when she realized what he was saying.

"I bought you flowers," he continued, "made dinner reservations..."

"I can explain."

"I'm sure you can. We'll talk in the morning. Think about what you're going to say. Make it good. Right now, I'm angry, drunk, and tired."

He went off to the spare room.

He didn't sleep well.

He got up later than usual and made a pot of coffee. His mouth was dry. His stomach was upset. His head was pounding. He had never been hungover before.

Lucy came down a little later. Her eyes were red from crying. She looked broken. She carried a box of tissues. She poured herself coffee and sat opposite Alex.

"Well," Alex said. "What's your story?"

"I don't have one. "

"How long has it been going on?"

"A few weeks." She sniffled and blew her nose. "It doesn't mean anything."

"Oh, I think it does. We haven't made love in six months."

"That can't be right." She tried to remember the last time. She couldn't.

"New Year's Eve," he said. "Would you stop if I asked you to?"

"Sure. Anything you want. I'm sorry."

He stood.

"I need to get my car. I left it at the bar."

"I'll take you."

"I'll walk. I don't want to be with you right now."

He went to the entryway and put on his shoes.

"I love you," Lucy called as he slammed the door.

Frank was in his front yard applying weed and feed with a spreader.

"Hey there, neighbor," Frank said.

"Frank."

"How's everything?"

"Oh, just peachy!" Alex said a little too loudly.

"Is something wrong?"

"Your wife—!" he stammered. His arms flailed.

Kay stepped outside.

"Hey, neighbor!"

"You!" Alex yelled, pointing at her. He stomped down the sidewalk, muttering to himself.

Frank gave Kay a stern look.

"Looks like the cat's out of the bag," she said.

How could Lucy do this to him? He had his faults but thought he'd been a good husband. He tried to give her everything she needed—a nice house, furniture, freedom. She'd never gone hungry unless she was doing Weight Watchers.

When he got back, the door to the master suite was closed. Lucy probably needed to be alone, too. That was a good thing.

He decided to break down the bed in the spare room and move it to his office in the basement. He tried to do it quietly, but it required some loud pounding with a mallet. He was pushing the mattress into the hall when he found Lucy blocking his way.

"What's going on?" she asked timidly. Her eyes were still red.

"I'm moving to the basement."

"Why?"

"So I won't irritate you with my presence."

"I'm not the one who's irritated. Let me help."

"I don't want your help. I'm too pissed."

"Then wait until you're not pissed."

It was the stupidest thing he'd ever heard.

"If I wait until I'm not pissed, I won't need to move the bed."

"Fine."

She stepped out of his way.

The basement was comfortable. He had everything he needed there: a toilet and shower, a big desk, a huge tv, and an incredible stereo that he hardly ever used.

The previous owners of the house had left a fully stocked wet bar with bottles of expensive liquor that had never been touched. That was going to change. He picked a bottle of Glen Fiddich and poured some into a whiskey glass. He took a sip and shivered. Well, he could probably get used to it.

He went to the desk, booted up the computer, and parsed website data. From time to time, he heard Lucy upstairs, footfalls on the floor, and pots and pans banging in the kitchen. Her presence upstairs was an annoying distraction.

He loaded up the carousel of his cd player with heavy metal and turned the volume up on the stereo.

Chapter 41

STRATEGY SESSION

Kay was sunbathing when Lucy met with her at their usual time. Lucy plopped down in the lounge chair next to her. Kay handed her a bottle of wine.

"Did you tell him, or did he find out some other way?" Kay asked.

"He came home early from work yesterday and caught us in the act."

"Ouch."

"Ouch, is right." Lucy took a drink.

"Are you okay?"

"No, I'm not okay!" She looked at Kay. "What do I do now?"

Kay thought for a moment. "You know, sex isn't everything. But I've found a good blowjob can go a long way in calming an angry man."

Chapter 42

PEACE OFFERING

Alex worked until his stomach growled with hunger. He looked at the time on the monitor. 9:30, nighttime. Time flew when you were angry and obsessed with your work.

He cautiously climbed the stairs.

The ground floor was dark. A dim light came from the dining room table. There was a candle, a single rose in a vase, and a covered plate of food— dinner for one.

The gesture was hard to appreciate under the circumstances. He sat and uncovered the plate—meatloaf, mashed potatoes, and a vegetable medley. He ate enough to quiet the rumble in his belly.

He stood and went to the front of the house. The stairway was lit with small candles, placed on dessert plates every few steps. He followed the candles up the stairs to the door of the master suite.

Lucy was lying on the bed, facing away from the door, naked, her body a peace offering. He wasn't so angry now.

He lay down and put his arm around her. She turned to face him and kissed him. She pulled her body into his.

"You don't have to," he said.

"I want to."

"I can't."

She sniffled. “I think I’m a lesbian.”

His heart sank. “This isn’t just...experimentation?”

“I thought people were exaggerating—the earth moving, fireworks going off. I have that with Kay.”

He groaned.

“Don’t be hurt,” she said. “It was always good with you, too.”

“So good we have sex twice a year.”

She didn’t know what to say.

“Do you love her?” he asked.

“I don’t know what this is with her. It's like I’m under some kind of spell. But I’m sure that I love you. Absolutely sure. You’re my soulmate. If I have to choose, I choose you.” She grabbed a tissue and blew her nose. He kissed her on the shoulder.

“Can you be happy that way?” he asked.

“I can be content.”

“Not good enough.”

“What do we do?”

“I think we have to move on. Go our separate ways.”

She started crying in earnest. It broke his heart. His anger was gone.

“We’ll talk more tomorrow,” he said.

He held her until she fell asleep.

Chapter 43
FORWARD

Alex spent most of his time in the basement.

Lucy continued seeing Kay. She felt guilty about the whole mess, but she couldn't quit. There wasn't a reason to. Alex had already decided on divorce.

They didn't tell anyone right away. They wanted time to make decisions. A few weeks passed, and Alex had a talk with Brad.

"Lucy's not going with me to the Landies," Alex told him.

"Oh?"

"Looks like we're getting a divorce."

"Sorry to hear that. I had a feeling." Alex wondered what had tipped him off. "Can you find someone else?"

"I can go by myself."

"I can't get a refund on the plane ticket. Pick someone. Anyone but Madison."

"She was my first choice."

"That's exactly why. You're asking for trouble. You're her superior."

"Technically, no. She reports to you."

"It's a bad idea."

"You're saying that because of the picnic. We were pulling your chain. We're just friends."

"Do you swear? Because what I saw sure looked convincing."

Alex crossed his heart.

"Ok, but if this blows up, it's on you," Brad said.

Madison was at her desk when Alex stopped by. He knocked on the doorway. She looked up and smiled. The asters he had bought for Lucy were in a vase on the corner of Madison's desk.

"Nice flowers," he said.

She shrugged. "They're second-hand."

"What are you doing the weekend of September 17th?"

Her smile grew as she looked at the calendar on her monitor. "Well, as it turns out, I'm free. What did you have in mind?"

"My date for the Landies can't make it. Would you like to go?"

She smiled. "I'd be delighted."

Chapter 44
MEDIATION

"Maybe we should see a marriage counselor," Lucy said one day.

"That won't change your gender preference," Alex said.

"No, I guess not."

Alex and Lucy decided on a no-fault divorce. They didn't have to pay for expensive lawyers that way.

Arbitration would do the job for a fraction of the cost. They'd sell the house and split the money 50-50. Alex's retirement fund would be tricky because he'd have to pay taxes. Handing the money over to the IRS rubbed him the wrong way, but there was no way around it.

His ownership in Tucker-Herman was tricky, too. Alex would have to transfer half of his shares to Lucy. That made Brad nervous. Lucy would own 25%. She could sell her shares, and Brad didn't want an outsider involved in the company. But Lucy assured them that she wouldn't sell. She could use the income every quarter when the profits were divvied up.

"I'll have to get a job, though," she told Alex. She laughed. "That Bachelor's in Fine Art is finally gonna come in handy."

"Oh boy," Alex said sarcastically.

Chapter 45
A CHAT WITH KAY

The hardest part for Alex was when Kay came to visit. Frank was obviously a tolerant guy, but he had one ironclad rule: Kay couldn't have any play-dates at their house while he was there, to make sure everyone stayed comfortable. That meant that Kay came over frequently to visit Lucy. It was usually not a problem, as it was easy for Alex to keep out of their way. Sometimes, though, Alex and Kay would raid the kitchen for a snack at the same time.

The first time this happened, it was awkward.

"Ah, there's the homewrecker," Alex said.

"I never wrecked a home that didn't need wrecking," Kay replied.

The second time, Kay said, "We should talk."

"Okay." Alex sat at the breakfast nook, and Kay sat across from him.

"I'm sorry," she said.

"Me, too."

"Lucy really loves you," Kay said.

Alex stared at her blankly.

"Do you still love her?" she asked.

"I don't know." He was too numb to feel anything. And if he ever felt love again, he doubted that he'd be able to admit it. It had been hard enough to say the first time, twenty years ago. And now? He felt like a fool.

"I'm going to make some predictions," Kay said. "Things are going to get better for you every day. The anger will fade. Someday you'll be able to forgive us. Someday you and I will be friends." She rose. "It's good when the people you love can love each other."

"Not everybody can be like you," he said.

She smiled.

"Well, that's a shame," she said.

She returned to the master suite to share a bed with his wife.

But things got better, just like Kay said they would.

Chapter 46

PIPE DREAM

One night after Alex came home from work, Lucy wanted to talk. It was late. She found him on a wicker loveseat in the backyard, drinking scotch and looking at the stars. He was having a pipe dream without the pipe.

"Do you mind some company?" she asked.

"No. Have a seat."

She produced a joint.

"Is that what I think it is?" he asked.

"Yeah. Want some?"

"Sure, why not?"

She lit it and took a drag. She handed it to Alex, who followed her example. She took his free hand and held it. He didn't pull away.

"Where'd you get it?" he asked.

"Kay. She says it's Joey Rossetti's. I have my doubts."

She took another puff.

"What's the most shocking thing you've ever experienced?" she asked him.

"Finding you and Kay. By far."

"Sorry."

"You don't have to keep apologizing. It's annoying."

"Sorry." She snickered. "Oops."

He smiled at her. He took the joint and took another drag. "What about you? Most shocking?"

She laughed. "When I found out how babies were made. I'd heard stories and didn't believe any of it. But they made us watch a cheesy movie in seventh grade that confirmed it all. I was like, 'The boy puts that thing in there?' And the implications— Mom and Dad had to do that to make me! I couldn't imagine! It was bananas!"

"It was a shock for me, too. But after the shock wore off, that's all I could think about."

They laughed together.

"I had a physical exam today," she said.

"Is everything ok?"

"Yeah. I told the doctor that I want to go off the Prozac."

"Are you sure?"

"I don't think I need it anymore."

"Please be careful."

"I will. They're going to wean me off over the next month."

"You know yourself better than anyone."

"I'm beginning to."

She kissed his hand and said goodnight.

Chapter 47

BON VOYAGE

"How are you getting to the airport?" Lucy asked as Alex packed for his trip to Seattle.

"I'm driving."

"You'll have to park in the long-term lot. That'll be expensive. Why don't I drive you?"

"You don't mind?"

"Not at all."

"Okay. One of my coworkers is going, too. Can we pick her up on the way?"

"I don't see why not." She didn't like the idea but couldn't articulate why, so she had no right to object. "Would that be Madison Lundquist?"

"Yeah. How did you know?"

"Just a guess."

Madison's apartment was on the way to the airport. She was waiting for them on the front porch with her suitcase. Alex made introductions after he put Madison's suitcase in the trunk.

"I think we've met," Madison said from the back seat.

"Oh?" said Lucy, pretending to forget.

"At the hospital, when Alex had his back surgery."

"I didn't see you at the hospital," Alex said.

"I dropped off flowers. You were asleep."

Did Madison know what was going on? Lucy wondered. About the divorce? It was hard to say. Alex wasn't much of a talker, especially when it came to unpleasant subjects. But the staff of Tucker-Herman loved some good gossip. The odds were fifty-fifty.

Lucy pulled up to the curb at the terminal and turned the car off. Alex and Madison hopped out and got their luggage out of the trunk. Lucy followed them to the curb.

"You two have a good trip," she said. "Be safe."

"Don't worry," Madison said. "I'll take good care of him."

That's precisely what Lucy was afraid of.

Alex wasn't sure how to say goodbye. He extended his hand for a handshake.

"Don't be an idiot," Lucy said. She hugged him. She waved as they turned and headed to the luggage check.

Lucy's heart sank. *Damn!* They looked like a couple.

Chapter 48
DEPARTURE

Alex and Madison had an hour before their flight boarded.

"I could use a drink," Alex said.

"Okay."

They rolled their carry-ons to a tiny place that served cocktails. Alex had a double scotch. Madison sipped on Perrier.

Alex fidgeted more than usual.

"Are you anxious?" Madison asked.

"I'm fine," he said.

He obviously wasn't fine.

They boarded, stowed their luggage in the overhead compartment, and got comfortable. Madison took the window seat. She noticed the tension in his face as the plane taxied to the runway.

"Flying makes you nervous," she said.

"Just the takeoff and landing. And the up in the air part."

"I know a trick," she said. "I know you don't like being touched. Do I have permission to touch you?"

"I actually enjoy being touched. But it has to be someone I like. And it helps if I have some warning."

"Do you like me?"

He smiled.

"You know I like you."

"Just wanted to make sure. Give me your hand." He placed his hand on hers, palm down. "Now close your eyes."

The plane's engines revved up. He closed his eyes. The muscles in his face tightened. She gently touched his hand with her index finger, tracing the outline of the palm, each finger, and thumb. He relaxed. She continued until the plane was high over the earth and the engines had throttled back.

"That wasn't so bad, was it?" she asked.

"No. I feel better. Thanks."

Madison fiddled with the movie screen in front of her when they were at cruising altitude.

"What would you like to do?" she asked. "Talk or watch a movie?"

"Let's talk."

"To have a conversation, we both have to participate."

"Okay."

"That's how conversations work."

"Yep. What do you want to talk about?"

"Let's see...what's happening with you and Lucy?"

"That was blunt."

"That's me. I don't beat around the bush."

He hesitated. "We're getting a divorce."

"We all knew something was up. You were 'drinking to forget' at the bar that night. You two have been together for a long time."

"Twenty years."

"Do you mind if I ask what happened?"

"She came to the conclusion, at the age of 41, that she's a lesbian."

Madison sat back.

"For real?"

"For real."

"That must have been a shock."

"Affirmative. It would make a good episode for The Jerry Springer Show—Lesbians and the Men Who Love Them."

"I think they actually did a show like that."

"So I'm not the only one? That's comforting," he said.

"Well, it could have been worse," she said. "At least you know it wasn't your fault. Divorce is bad enough without your ego getting bruised."

"It still hurts."

"I know. My divorce was rough. But looking back, it wasn't as bad as the marriage. I came out better than ever. You're going to be okay."

She looked out the window.

"Oh! Lake Michigan." She looked ahead. "And there's Wisconsin, my home state."

He leaned her way to look out the window. He had to press lightly against her to see.

She didn't seem to mind.

Chapter 49
SEATTLE

They were staying at the same hotel where the awards banquet was being held. When they tried to check in, they ran into a problem—there was only one room. The arrangements had been made before Lucy's Big Surprise. There was so much chaos in Alex's life that he forgot to book a room for Madison. Tonight, there were no vacancies.

They sat in the lobby and searched the internet for another room. The choices were few.

"Here's a room ten minutes away," she said.

"Inconvenient, but doable."

"Nope. Only two stars."

"That's fine. I'll take it."

"Listen," she said. "I think we should stick together. I'm a single girl in a strange town."

"What are you suggesting?"

"That we share the room here."

"Are you okay with that?"

"I'm okay if you're okay. We're grown-ups. We don't have to let our hormones run amok."

"Ha-ha. Funny." The only hormones that ever ran amok with him were stress hormones. "There's only one bed."

"Yeah, a king. You stay on your side, and I'll stay on mine."

"Are you sure?" he asked.

"Yes."

They went back to the desk and checked in.

In the elevator, the humor of the situation struck Alex. "Brad'll have a seizure when he finds out we're sharing a room."

"That could be fun. We could watch him flop around a while before we call an ambulance."

"Let's not tell him."

"Chicken."

They wheeled their luggage into the room. Alex removed his shoes and lay on the bed to get a feel of the mattress. Madison opened the drapes.

"Nice view," she said.

"I hope so. Tucker-Herman paid extra for that."

She opened the refrigerator.

"Two bottles of Dom Perignon."

"Yeah, I'm paying for that myself. This was supposed to be a romantic getaway."

She wandered into the bathroom.

"Ah! A jacuzzi! That bathtub and I have a date tonight."

"Feel free." He was sad. "All of this was for Lucy."

"She'll never know what she missed." She grabbed her purse. "I'm going shopping. I brought a dress, but now I'm thinking I need something more glamorous."

"It's the Landies, not the Oscars."

"Let me indulge myself. Want to come along?"

"No. I'm going to take a little nap, I think. I need some quiet time after that flight."

"Okay. I won't be gone long."

The banquet was to start at 7. At 6, Madison hadn't come back yet. Alex was worried until she texted him, saying she was on her way and that he should start getting dressed. He shaved, showered, and was getting ready to put on his suit jacket when there was a knock on the door. He looked at his watch. 6:40. He opened the door to find Madison in a black strapless dress. She turned and posed like a fashion model.

"Wow," he said. "Look at you."

"You're looking pretty sharp yourself, mister. Come on," she said. She helped him with his jacket and straightened his tie.

The banquet hall was crowded. The audience ranged in age from teenagers to people in their 80s. Clothing ran the gamut from t-shirts and jeans to tuxedos.

"Let's get a table in the back," said Alex. He was a back-row kind of guy.

"I believe it's assigned seating," Madison said. She led him by the hand to a table in the front row. She picked up a place marker. "That seat's yours. I'll be Lucy tonight."

"I hate these things," Alex said. "Brad says I don't have to network. Then why am I here?"

"I don't know."

They sat as the MC took the podium. There were the usual greetings, thanks to the sponsors and hosts, and a brief history of the organization.

Alex looked at Madison. She was stunning. He forgot where he was for a moment. She looked back at him and smiled. He came back to reality when the MC began announcing the awards.

She got her phone out and punched buttons on the screen.

"Who are you calling?" he asked.

"Brad wanted me to put this on a Zoom call."

"If he wanted to see it, why didn't he come himself?"

Madison smiled and shrugged.

"I smell a rat," said Alex.

He heard Brad's voice on Madison's phone.

"Hey, Madison."

"Brad."

Then he heard Garth. "Madison. Looking good!"

"Thank you," she said.

"Is everyone on Zoom?" Alex asked.

"Yep."

Then he heard Lilith. "Hey, girlfriend! Love the dress!"

"Isn't it amazing?"

The MC said, "And now for the lifetime achievement award for contributions to the science and art of search engine optimization, Alex Herman!"

Everyone applauded. Alex's jaw dropped.

"Surprise!" said Madison."

"You knew!" said Alex as he got to his feet.

She nodded and grinned. She held up her phone so their friends could see Alex head to the podium.

He couldn't remember much of it afterward, but somehow he made it to the podium and accepted the award. He thanked the giants of technology before him. He mentioned Grace Hopper, Ted Nelson, Marc Andreeson, and Larry Page. Madison beamed proudly. Then he ran out of words and returned to the table.

•♥•♥•♥•♥•♥•

After the banquet, they walked arm-in-arm through the lobby, as sophisticated couples do at fancy events. Madison carried the award.

A young man greeted them by the front desk.

"Mr. Herman, I'm a big fan. I've read all of your white papers."

Alex blushed. "I don't know what to say. I'm surprised anyone knows who I am."

"Can I get a picture with you and Mrs. Herman?" the young man asked.

"Oh, I'm not Mrs. Herman," Madison said. "I'm his mistress." She laughed and looked at Alex for his reaction.

"Troublemaker," he said. "Sure, get in here."

The young man held up his phone, with Madison and Alex flanking him, and took a selfie. He thanked them and continued down the hall.

"That was fun," Madison said. "Would you like to go to the after-party?"

"I'll go if you go."

"On second thought, it's been a big day. I think I'm ready for bed. It's after one in Michigan."

"Sounds good."

When they got back to the room, Madison had him unzip her dress for her.

"What do you sleep in?" she asked.

"Boxers and T-shirt. I didn't bring pajamas."

"Only nerds wear pajamas."

"Well..." He smiled. "How about you?"

"Booty shorts and T-shirt. Is that okay? I don't want you to be uncomfortable."

"That's fine."

She went to the bathroom to brush her teeth and change. He took off his suit.

"I'm exhausted," she said. "That jacuzzi will have to wait until tomorrow, if we have time. When do we board?"

"Eight-thirty am."

"Oh, pooh."

"Monday."

"What?"

"This was supposed to be a long romantic weekend before... you know."

"Nice. Maybe we can do some sightseeing tomorrow." She came out of the bathroom in her t-shirt and booty shorts. "All done. Minty fresh." She blew on his face so he could smell her breath. "Your turn."

When he came back to the bed, she was under the covers. He pulled the covers back and climbed in next to her.

"Did you brush your teeth?" she asked.

He faced her and blew a breath in her direction.

"Acceptable," she said. She turned out the light on the nightstand. "Goodnight."

The smell of fresh coffee woke him the following day. He sat up, rubbed the sleep out of his eyes, and looked around the room. Madison looked out the window, watching the rain pour, holding the cup of coffee, still in her booty shorts and T-shirt.

He was happy that she was with him. He had known her only a few months but was comfortable with her. Again, she reminded him of someone. He couldn't figure out who.

"Good morning," she said. "Want coffee?"

"Yeah, thanks," he said. "I have to use the bathroom."

"Don't let me stop you."

"Could you turn around, please?"

She turned away.

"What did you have planned for today?" she asked.

He came back into the room, drying his face.

"Couples massage at one. The art museum afterward. Dinner at the Space Needle at seven."

"Sounds good. Let's do it."

"Which part?"

"All of it."

They took turns showering and dressing and had breakfast in the hotel restaurant. By the time they were through with breakfast, it was raining hard. The air was chilly. They stood under the hotel portico, trying to decide if it was worth the trouble to go out again.

"Did you bring a raincoat?" Alex asked.

"No."

"Neither did I. Well, we only have two hours before the couples massage."

"Back to the room?"

"Back to the room."

They had two bottles of good champagne to amuse themselves with. It was almost noon, which wasn't too early for champagne, they figured. And it was a good way to relax before the massage.

They sat on the bed.

"I'm looking forward to this massage," Madison said. "It's been a while."

"I've never had one," Alex said. He had wondered what it was like but couldn't deal with the thought of a stranger touching him like that.

"You're in for a treat."

"I don't know. It's weird."

"Why?"

"It's a couples massage. We're not a couple."

"Close enough. We're two people who enjoy each others' company."

They rode the elevator to the hotel spa. They checked in, and the attendant led them to a dimly lit room that had two massage tables and smelled of essential oils. The relaxing sound of a wooden flute played on the stereo. The attendant closed the door behind her as she left.

Madison started disrobing.

"What do I do?" Alex asked.

"Take off your clothes, silly."

Alex unbuttoned his shirt. *"All* my clothes?"

Madison folded her dress and placed it on a bench. "It's up to you, but less clothing makes for a better massage. I won't look." She took off her bra and placed it on her folded dress.

He briefly saw the fall of her breasts before he could turn away. He tried not to think about her body. He didn't want to get stimulated in an awkward way.

"Lie down and put your face in the middle of that donut thing," Madison said. "Cover yourself with the sheet. Relax and focus on the sensation."

There was a knock on the door.

"We're ready," Madison called out.

Two masseuses came into the room and began their work. Alex felt warm oil applied to his neck, hands rubbing the oil in, kneading, and working down to his shoulders. In a few minutes, he got over the feeling of awkwardness and was able to enjoy it.

Madison sighed with pleasure a few times.

Halfway through, his masseuse told him it was time to turn over. She lifted the sheet and looked away while he flipped onto his back. He drifted off to sleep.

He woke to the voice of his masseuse in his right ear, whispering, "All done." The two masseuses quietly left the room, closing the door behind them.

He laid still for a minute, then looked at Madison. She was lying on her side, smiling at him.

"Well?" she asked.

"Why did I wait so long for that?"

"The whole thing about being touched by strangers, probably."

They got dressed in silence. Before they left the salon, Madison said, "Leave a nice tip."

Alex got his wallet out and handed two twenty-dollar bills to the attendant. "Thank you," he said.

As they approached the elevator, Madison took his hand.

"What now?" Alex asked. He looked at his watch. "The art museum?"

"Maybe later. Right now, I want to go back to the room and enjoy the mellow."

They returned to the room, took off their shoes, and lay on the bed. Alex closed his eyes. Madison snuggled against him and put her hand on his chest.

"What happened to staying on your side of the bed?" he asked.

"Oops. Sorry," she said. "Old habits."

Alex woke again to the smell of fresh coffee. Madison was standing at the window, in a bra and panties, coffee in hand.

"Nice view?" he asked.

"Yes," she said.

The view was nice from his vantage, too.

"What time is it?"

"Four-thirty. The art museum is off the table. It closes at five. You looked so peaceful I didn't want to wake you."

"That's a shame."

"Maybe we'll get another chance someday."

"If we get to the Space Needle early, we can take in the view before dinner."

She agreed.

"What should I wear?"

"You looked good in your suit last night. You should wear it again."

"Okay. If you wear the dress."

"I might not get another opportunity."

Chapter 50
DINNER

Madison was frustrated on the ride to The Space Needle. She had been mildly attracted to Alex when they first met, and the attraction had grown over the last few months. But he was married, off limits. Madison was a nice girl, or so she liked to think. She couldn't set her sights on a married man. She knew what it was like to be the victim of a cheater.

She knew he liked her, but how far did it go? Was it shyness? Lack of confidence? Maybe he was asexual. That would be unfortunate. Maybe he just wasn't into her that way.

Everyone at Tucker-Herman suspected his marriage was in trouble, and now that she knew divorce was on the horizon, that gave her the green light. She had pulled out every trick she knew to seduce him short of telling him bluntly that she wanted to have sex with him. The hand thing on the plane. The dress that cost a week's salary. The "mistress" joke outside the banquet room, maybe less of a joke than wishful thinking. The touches on the arm, the makeup, the perfume. They slept in the same bed, for crying out loud, and he hadn't touched her. Parading around the room in her bra and panties, which was a show she didn't put on for just any guy. No reaction. It was admirable and maddening at the same time.

It just wasn't right.

It was chilly when they got to the observation deck of the Space Needle. She shivered and cuddled against him as they looked eastward to that amazing view of The Cascades, and Mount Rainier to the south. Her teeth chattered. He looked into her eyes, then back to the mountain range. He unbuttoned his suit jacket and took it off. He draped it over her shoulders and pulled her into him. She rested her head on his chest.

Wow! Finally! she thought. *Something!*

They stood like that, silently taking in the view and each others' warmth until it was time for dinner.

The food was fantastic. The conversation was intimate. They talked about their childhood interests, the music they liked, dating catastrophes in college, marriage, and divorce.

On the cab ride back to the hotel, Alex offered his hand for her to hold. That was another big step. It was like high school all over again, warm and innocent.

Chapter 51
DESSERT

In the hotel room, Madison said, "Could you unzip me again?"

He obliged. She held up her dress with one hand and went to the bathroom to disrobe.

"What do you want to do now?" he asked her.

"We have another bottle of champagne. Why don't you open it while I try out the jacuzzi?"

He opened the champagne while she filled the tub. She sang as she undressed, an improvised melody with nonsense words, the sounds of a happy woman. She stepped into the tub, lay in the water, and started the jets. After a moment, she turned the jets off.

"Alex?"

"Yeah?"

"Did you open the champagne yet?"

"Yes."

"Could you bring some to me?"

"Sure thing. Hold on."

A minute later, he entered the bathroom, the champagne flute in one hand and the other hand covering his eyes. He held the flute out, walking blindly. She laughed.

"Say something so I can navigate," he said.

"This way. Warmer. Warmer. That's it." She reached out and took the flute from him. "Thank you."

"You're welcome."

"Give me half an hour. Think of something to do when I get out."

"I'll try."

He went back to the bedroom. Madison turned the jets on again.

After half an hour, she turned off the jets, opened the drain, stepped out, and toweled off. She donned the plush bathrobe the hotel provided and entered the bedroom.

Alex was staring at his phone.

"Still looking," he said.

"Any ideas?"

"Nothing that stands out."

Time was running out for her. It was a bold move. She loosened the belt to her bathrobe, opened it, and let it fall to the floor.

"How about now?" she asked.

Something began to stand out in his slacks, and he was full of ideas. His fingers flew, working the buttons of his shirt.

"Can I help you with that?" she asked.

"Yes, please."

She pulled him out of his shirt.

"I'd like to kiss you. Is that okay?"

"Yes."

He was a good kisser despite the slow start.

"Could you lie back for me?"

He did.

"Can I kiss your neck?"

"Yes."

She straddled him and buried her head in the curve of his neck. Her hair fell around his face like a veil.

"Can I lick your ear?"

"Yes, yes to all of it."

Good. Total surrender. At last.

She loosened his belt, unzipped his fly, and pulled his slacks and boxers off his legs.

His cock sprang free and into the air. The sight made her happy. Now there was no doubt that he was into her.

She caressed him as they kissed. The sounds he made told her he was enjoying this as much as she was, but his hands were passive. That wasn't working for her.

"You can touch me, too," she said.

"What if I do something you don't like?"

"I'm going to love everything you do. I promise."

His hands stroked her sides gently and gradually got more adventurous.

"That's right," she said. "Just like that."

A hand came up and felt her breast.

"Mmm, I like that." She offered that breast to his lips, and he kissed it. He licked her nipple, then sucked it gently. His hands were moving over her body freely now.

She was delighted to find that he knew where her clitoris was and what to do when he got there.

She grabbed his cock and put him into her, literally now. She posted slowly, rocking her pelvis. His hands gripped her ass and pulled as he pushed himself into her.

He made the sounds and the face that let her know he was getting close. Too soon. He probably hadn't had sex in a long time, but neither had she.

"Hang on, baby, I'm right behind you," she said.

He tried to hold off but failed. He spasmed one, two, three times.

"I'm sorry," he said. But he was still hard.

"Don't stop. I'm almost there.

He flipped them over, and then he was on top, thrusting, taking charge in a way that surprised her. Her legs wrapped around his waist, pulling him deep into her on the downstroke.

"Yes!" she said.

He bowed his head, caught her left nipple in his teeth, and nipped gently. That sent her over the edge.

Kaboom!

After waking the following day, she stayed in bed for a while and watched her man sleep.

Her man?

That was premature.

Careful, girl!

Alex wasn't the kind of guy she saw herself falling for. But here they were. It had been building for a while and didn't make any sense at all.

She hadn't had sex in a long time. That's what this was all about—raging hormones. They could be fuck buddies for a while, and that was okay. It would be good until it wasn't, then they'd move on—the story of her life.

She'd been in a bad situation when she met Alex, and he rescued her. She remembered a lesson from one of her psych classes—she was like one of Lorenz's newly hatched geese, imprinting on the first friendly creature that came along.

She could come up with excuses all day long. She needed to protect herself.

She put on the bathrobe and made coffee. She put a cup on his nightstand and said, "Time to wake up, baby."

He woke slowly. She wandered to the window and took in the view.

"You're here," he said, half asleep.

"Of course. Where else would I be?"

"I thought it was a dream." He smiled.

"Nope. IRL." In Real Life.

"Kathleen Sears!" he said suddenly.

"Who?"

"My first crush. I've been trying to figure out who you remind me of."

"She must have been awesome."

"I never met her. She was a lingerie model in the Sears catalog. I remember a picture of her in a bathrobe. You're the spitting image."

Madison smiled. "Let me get this straight—I remind you of your teenage masturbation fantasy?"

He blushed. "Yeah," he confessed.

She laughed. "Well, maybe I can pose for you sometime while you pleasure yourself." His blush deepened. She had embarrassed him. "Maybe after we get to know each other better," she said.

She returned to the bed and drank her coffee beside him.

He sipped in silence for a while. He turned pensive. He sighed.

"What?" she asked.

"Do you have a fetish for older men?" he asked. "Daddy issues, maybe?"

"Maybe," she said. She considered. "No. I have a fetish for intelligence, maturity, and kindness."

He brooded for a while, then asked, "Do you think this is going to last?"

"Like I'll dump you if someone else comes along?"

"Yeah, the thought occurred to me. I'm a little gun-shy right now."

"Me, too."

"Last night was amazing."

"And today will be as well."

She got a smile out of him.

"This is happening fast," he said. "I think this could really hurt."

She took his hand and looked him in the eyes. "Did anybody ever tell you that you think too much?"

"All the time."

She kissed his hand.

"This is new," she said. "It can be anything we want it to be. Let's keep it casual for now. It's too soon to get serious. But let's enjoy it for a while before we throw a wet blanket on it."

She kissed him. Before they knew it, they were making love again. They came together this time, and it was magic. But there was no time for cuddling.

"Let's get moving," Madison said. "We've got a plane to catch."

They showered together. Alex *radiated.* He didn't have a problem with being touched by her anymore. He didn't have a problem touching her. They would have made love in the shower again if there had been more time. They lathered each other, rinsed each other off, and took turns drying each other.

They watched each other dress without modesty or shame.

They held hands in the taxi on the way to the airport. They looked out the window silently, taking mental pictures of Seattle as they said goodbye to the city.

Before they got to the airport, Madison said, "I have a confession to make."

"Please don't tell me you're a lesbian."

She laughed. "No. Brad asked me to book another room five weeks ago. I forgot. On purpose."

He looked at her. "Oh, well. It turned out okay." He smiled.

"Just okay?" She punched him lightly in the arm.

"You hit like a girl," he said.

She punched him again, harder this time.

"Ow," he said.

Chapter 52

TRIUMPHANT RETURN

Lucy met them at the airport after the plane landed. She wasn't happy about it, but what could she do? She had relinquished any right to jealousy when she cheated on Alex, as Kay reminded her. Lucy was determined to be civilized.

The text from him said, "Delta Air door 5". She pulled up to the door, and there they were. She got out and opened the rear hatch to the SUV.

"How was Seattle?" she asked.

"It was amazing," said Madison. She was glowing. They both were glowing. Lucy hadn't seen Alex like this since they started dating twenty years ago. Lucy's heart sank. She knew they had been intimate. It was official—they really were a couple now.

Alex put their luggage into the vehicle while Madison hopped into the back seat. Alex got into the back seat with her.

"My God, I feel like a chauffeur," said Lucy.

"Sorry," Madison said, and she sat beside Lucy.

Lucy eased into traffic. "Tell me all about it. Where did you go? What did you see?"

"Oh, you know," Madison said. "Dinner at the Space Needle."

"That's it?"

"Yeah. We stayed in the hotel almost the whole time," said Madison.

"Oh?" said Lucy. It sounded judgmental. Lucy couldn't help it.

"We had a couple's massage," Alex offered without thinking. There followed a silence that was even more awkward. "I won a Landy award," he said.

"Well, good for you," said Lucy, with enthusiasm complicated by other emotions.

No one spoke again until they reached Madison's apartment.

Lucy popped the rear hatch, and Alex helped Madison to the porch with her bags. They stood on the porch, hugging and swapping saliva, looking into each other's eyes.

"What are you?" Lucy said to herself. "Teenagers?"

After an eternity, they finally uncoupled, and Alex climbed into the passenger's seat.

"She's young," Lucy said.

"She's older than she looks," Alex replied.

"Things are moving kind of fast."

"I know."

"Do you think it'll last?"

"Probably not."

The next day at work, Madison sat in her usual chair in the conference room. Alex walked in a few minutes later with his Landy, holding it high.

"Congratulations," Brad said. "Let's see it."

Alex handed the trophy to Brad, who passed it around.

Alex sat in the chair opposite Madison instead of next to her, thinking he was being discreet. Madison smiled at him warmly. He returned the smile. She looked at the empty chair to her left, then back at him, teasing him.

Everyone noticed. He realized too late that he wasn't being discreet at all.

Chapter 53

SOMETHING LIKE ROMANCE

After work, Madison FaceTimed her sister Colleen. It had been a few weeks since they had talked, and now Madison had something to report. Colleen accepted the call, and it took a few seconds to get her phone oriented so they could see each other.

"Hey, sis," Colleen said. "You're looking good. How's the job going?"

"Great. I just got back from an awards ceremony. In Seattle."

"Seattle? How was it?"

"Had a good time. One of the owners won an award."

"What's with you?"

"What do you mean?"

"You're all...giddy." Colleen sounded suspicious. "Did everybody go?"

"No. Just me and the boss."

"Ah," Colleen said. "Let me ask you this, and you don't have to tell me, but you should because I'm your sister, and I love you very much—did anything like romance occur on this trip to Seattle?"

"I wouldn't call it romance. But *something like* romance would be accurate."

"So you had a good time."

"I had a great time."

"Is it serious?"

"Oh, no. We're just being casual."

"Are you sure?"

"Sure, I'm sure. It's the 21st century. A girl can have healthy sex with no strings attached."

"I know, I know. We've both been there and, God willing, I'll get there again. But you've had a fair number of partners before, and I've met a few of them. I've only seen you like this one other time—when you started dating Voldemort."

"Lars?"

"Yes, Lars. This doesn't look like casual to me. And that's fine. But be careful. Don't get hurt again."

"You're wrong— "

"If you say so— "

"—but I'll keep that in mind. Love you, sis. Gotta go."

"Love you, too. Talk to you soon."

Chapter 54

A CHAT WITH HANNAH

"What a mess," Alex said.

Lucy sat across from him at the breakfast nook. It was time to update Hannah on recent events. Alex dreaded the conversation. He covered his face with his hands.

"I'm sorry," Lucy said. She screwed up her face and clenched her fists on the table.

"What are you doing?"

"Trying to turn straight," she said. It was an attempt to lighten the mood.

"Very funny. Is it working?"

She rolled her eyes up as if looking into her own mind.

"Nope. Still queer," she said.

Alex laughed despite the circumstances. He patted her hand. "Well, keep trying. There's still hope."

Hannah came in."What did you want to see me about?" she asked.

Lucy moved over so Hannah could sit. Lucy took in a deep breath.

"We have to tell you something," she said. "You might find it ...disturbing."

"You're getting a divorce," Hannah said.

"Well, that was easy," Alex said.

"How did you know?" asked Lucy.

"Are you kidding?" Hannah said. "I live in the same house as you, and I'm not stupid. Dad moved into the basement. You don't have dinner together anymore. Sometimes he doesn't even come home after work."

"Do you have any questions?" asked Lucy.

"Yes. Are we moving? I'd like to graduate from Pioneer, if possible."

"We're not moving right away. Your father and I still care about each other very much, and I think we can all get along under the same roof for a while."

Hannah let this sink in.

Hannah looked at Alex. "Did you decide on a divorce before or after you started banging Madison?"

"Before," Alex replied without thinking. "Hey, who says I'm banging Madison?"

"Sorry, Dad. I thought you were just being a typical male."

"You're forgiven." He waved it off. "But wait! There's more!" He gestured for Lucy to continue. Lucy was reluctant. "She needs to know," Alex prodded.

"Well," Lucy began, "you know how most people are attracted to people of the opposite gender?"

"You're a lesbian!" Hannah said. "You and Kay! Oh, my God, this explains so much. When did you figure it out?"

"Just recently."

"Well, good for you." Hannah stood. "I've got to go and wrap my head around all this. Thanks for the chat. I love you guys."

Hannah left the room, shaking her head at the strangeness of it all.

"That went better than expected," Alex said.

"She doesn't seem traumatized at all," Lucy replied.

Chapter 55
AN INVITATION

Over the next few weeks, Alex and Madison spent a lot of time together. After work, Alex usually went straight to Madison's apartment, not coming home until late, if at all. And why not? Lucy reasoned. They were new lovers, doing what new lovers do. This kind of thing was more than sex, was more than lust, but didn't always involve love. Kay called it New Relationship Energy. It was one of the reasons Lucy fell so hard for Kay. NRE was like a drug— intoxicating, addictive, and hard to tame.

Lucy understood all of this, but it still annoyed her. It threw her life off-kilter, not knowing when or if Alex would be home for dinner. She had been Mrs. Alex Herman for so long that she didn't know what to do with herself between playdates with Kay. Keeping a house only took a few hours a day. Hannah provided some companionship, but she was an active senior in high school with plenty to do, driving herself to the places she had to go, not eager for her square mother to tag along. Lucy had an empty space in her life again. Kay had filled one, but Alex's absence was creating another.

Thank goodness she had painting.

One day, Alex came home to work in the basement, and Lucy had a chance to speak with him.

"Are you eating okay?" she asked.

"We do a lot of dining out, but I'm not starving."

"I was thinking—why don't you invite Madison for dinner sometime?"

"Why?" he asked.

"I'd like to get to know her."

Alex was skeptical. "I'll ask, but I don't know. It's a little weird."

He was right, but life was weird now, and it looked like it would be that way for a while. Better to just embrace it.

He said he'd ask.

Madison, to Alex's surprise, accepted the invitation.

"Are you sure?" Alex asked.

"It has to be done. Might as well get it over with."

"But why?"

"It would be different if you hated each other and were making a clean break. But you don't, and you're not. She wants to check me out and see how she measures up. I guess it's an ego thing. I want to check her out, too."

They decided on a Saturday night.

"I'm putting together a menu," Lucy said Friday when she saw Alex. "Any requests?"

"No arsenic," Alex replied.

"Funny. I'm not using anything stronger than garlic," Lucy said. "I promise."

Alex and Madison spent the Saturday morning together, and then Madison shooed him away.

"I've got to get ready for battle," she said.

That made Alex uneasy, wondering what "battle" might consist of, so he did what he usually did with unsettling thoughts—he tried to ignore them.

When he got home, wonderful smells were wafting out of the kitchen. He went straight to the basement to stay out of Lucy's way.

The doorbell rang a little after six. He got a text from Lucy that said, "Could you get the door?"

He climbed the basement stairs.

The doorbell rang again just before he got to it. There was Madison in a fancy cocktail dress.

"For a second, I thought no one was home," she said.

"I was working in the basement," Alex said. "Um, the dress. Isn't it a bit much?"

"I'll be the judge of that."

Alex shrugged.

Then Lucy came into the entryway. "Welcome," she said.

Damned if she wasn't wearing a fancy dress, too. She never dressed like this. It was starting to look like a runway model competition.

. "Nice house," Madison said. "It's even more beautiful on the inside."

"Lucy did everything," Alex said.

"It's like a work of art," said Madison. It was the perfect thing to say to get on Lucy's good side.

"Thank you," Lucy said. "I have to finish in the kitchen. Go on in and have a seat. Bread and wine are on the table."

"Do you need any help?" Madison asked.

"No, it's almost ready."

"What are we having? It smells amazing."

"Just a simple pot roast."

Alex led Madison into the dining room. The table was all laid out with the good china. Two lit candles. A centerpiece with fresh flowers. A salad and a pot of soup were already waiting, with a loaf of fresh bread on a cutting board and a bottle of red wine.

"You can start without me," Lucy called from the kitchen. "I'll be right in."

Alex cut the bread into thick slices and passed the cutting board to Madison. She took a piece and tasted it.

"Mmm," she said, closing her eyes. "It tastes even better than it smells."

"Yeah, Lucy's quite a cook."

Alex poured three glasses of wine, and Lucy came in with sliced pot roast.

"Alex, could I borrow your propane torch?"

That came out of nowhere. "Why?"

"It's a surprise."

Alex sighed. "I'll get it for you."

He went to the garage and found the torch in the bottom drawer of his tool chest. He went to the kitchen and handed it to Lucy. She had a half-dozen ramekins with creme brulee ready for caramelizing.

"You don't have to do all this," he said.

"I feel like I do," she said. "Could you take the vegetables to the dining room?"

"Yep. Please don't burn the house down."

Lucy had made creme brulee many times before but had never torched the tops. That had always seemed like an extra step that didn't matter. Now things were going too far. Lucy was taking the competition beyond clothes and makeup.

Alex returned to the dining room with Pyrex dishes of asparagus tips and stuffed portabellas. He sat next to Madison, obviously irritated.

"What's the matter?" Madison asked.

"This was supposed to be a relaxed thing where you and Lucy could get to know each other."

"Yeah, she's a little over the top."

"You're not helping."

She looked at her dress.

"I was just trying to make a good impression."

"You and Lucy both. What's the point if you're putting on a show?"

"Where do you keep your clothes?"

"In the basement now."

"Show me."

He led her down the stairs to the basement.

"Unzip me, please," she said. He was happy to comply with that request, as always. She took off the dress and found a hanger to put it on.

"Don't just stand there. I need a T-shirt and a pair of sweatpants."

She went to the basement bathroom to wash off her makeup. He rummaged through some moving boxes and handed her what she asked for when she returned.

"They're wrinkled," he said.

"Perfect. You should change, too." She snapped her fingers. "Get with the program, buster."

He removed his dockers and polo shirt. He put on a t-shirt and sweats that were even more wrinkled than Madison's.

"Now, mess up my hair," Madison said.

"With pleasure." He ran his hands through her hair and tousled it. "Now kiss me," she said, and he did.

They returned to the dining room and drank wine as if nothing had changed.

Lucy came out and was ready to eat. Their change of clothes took her by surprise.

"What's going on, you two?" she asked.

"We weren't comfortable," Madison said. "This bread is incredible. sourdough?"

Lucy nodded. "I've got my own special culture." She looked down at her plate. "Excuse me. I think I'm overdressed."

She left the room, and Alex smiled. He grabbed Madison's hand. "Now we're on the right track."

Lucy returned in a pair of jean shorts and a tank top.

"There," she said. "That's better. I feel more relaxed already."

"Me, too," Alex said.

During the meal, the conversation was pleasant. Madison had expected an interrogation or battle of egos. But Lucy was friendly to her, considering Madison's new role as "the other woman."

Lucy asked Madison if she could cook, making Madison feel slightly inadequate. "I can't cook my way out of a paper bag," she confessed.

"What do you eat? You look healthy."

"Lots of salad. Raw veggies, the occasional boiled egg. I went straight from college to working seven days a week. Now that I have a decent job, I might have time to learn."

Alex was happy to see that they were getting along. It's good when the people you love can love each other. Kay had said that.

Toward the end of dinner, Lucy said, "Time for the torch."

"She made creme brulee," Alex said.

Madison got excited. "Oh! Can I watch?"

"Sure. Follow me," Lucy said.

She led them to the kitchen, opened the refrigerator, and pulled out the tray of ramekins. She set it on the kitchen island and sprinkled sugar over the tops of them. She grabbed the torch. After a few failed attempts to light it, she handed it to Alex.

Alex lit the torch and handed it back to Lucy. He got the fire extinguisher out of the pantry, just in case. Lucy adjusted the flame and waved it slowly over a ramekin until the sugar on top started to brown.

"Easy," Lucy said.

"Can I do one?" Madison asked.

"Sure." Lucy handed the torch to Madison.

Madison browned the top of hers the same way Lucy had done. The results were comparable. Madison felt gratified.

When the dessert had been eaten, the wine had been drunk, and the words had dwindled, Madison decided it was time to go.

"I'll clean up," she said.

"Nonsense," said Lucy. "You're our guest. I did the cooking. Alex gets to clean."

Alex nodded. "That's the way we do things. Let me get your dress, and I'll walk you to the door." When he returned, Madison was waiting in the entryway.

"That went okay," he said.

"She's good people," Madison said. "I can see why you were in love with her."

"Still am," he said, not thinking. An expression flashed across Madison's face that he couldn't decipher. Then she smiled. She stood against him and raised her head for a kiss.

"See you tomorrow," she said.

Alex went to the dining room and began clearing the table. Lucy was already loading the dishwasher.

"What did you think?" he asked.

"She's really pretty," Lucy said. "And smart. I think you've found the perfect rebound girl."

That sounded catty even to Alex, who wasn't good with social cues.

"You think that's all it is? Rebound sex?"

"Of course. What do *you* think it is?"

"I don't know." Which was true.

"Well, you'd better figure it out. I don't want you to get hurt."

"Again," he said. She looked at him blankly. "You don't want me to get hurt *again.*" He was angry. "Go to bed. I'll finish this. I'd like to be alone."

Chapter 56
THE MAGIC STICK

The staff was having lunch one day when Madison's phone announced the arrival of a new text message. She picked up the phone and looked at the screen.

"Huh!" she said.

"What?" Alex asked.

"Lars. His band's playing at The Magic Stick Saturday. He's asking me if I'd like to come."

The Magic Stick was a music venue in Detroit that was a landmark. Playing there was mandatory if you were a rock group with ambition.

"You're not going?" Alex said —half statement, half question.

"Of course not," she said. She thought about it while she chewed her food. "At least, not by myself." She looked intensely into Alex's eyes.

"Your Jedi mind tricks won't work with me," Alex said.

"Nothing?" she asked.

Alex shook his head.

She pouted.

"That's better," he said. "But still, no."

"Come on! You're a metalhead."

"I used to be a metalhead. At a distance. Why do you want to go? Haven't you had enough of that guy?"

"Maybe we can make him jealous."

"I can't imagine making anyone jealous."

Madison made her signature cry of exasperation. "Oof!" She addressed her coworkers. "Does anyone want to go to the Magic Stick with me?"

"Your ex's band," Bob said. "Are they any good?"

"No, but it doesn't matter," Madison said. "I'm buying pitchers."

Suddenly, everyone in the break room was interested. Then Alex agreed to go. It was what a good boyfriend should do. And he loved the look on her face when she got her way.

On Saturday night, Alex picked up Madison first. She sat in the passenger's seat and kissed him on the cheek.

"Why are we doing this again?" he asked.

"I feel like showing Lars some support. He says he's been clean for a couple of months. This is my way of rewarding him."

"Like a rat in a behaviorist experiment."

"Yes, exactly like that."

"Now tell me the real reason we're going."

Madison paused. "I want to show him that I'm doing okay. That I'm better off without him."

"If he's the asshole you say he is, just make a clean break. Never see him again."

Madison considered.

"Naw," she said.

They met Lilith, Garth, and Bob in the Tucker-Herman parking lot.

"Play them something," Alex said after their coworkers got into the back seat. "Give them a preview."

Madison plugged her phone into the USB port of Alex's stereo and cued up a song. A wailing, distorted guitar came out of the speakers, and drums sounding like a cross between a machine gun and a jackhammer. Then came angry, guttural vocals.

Garth laughed. "The vocalist sounds like Cookie Monster."

"You're right!" Madison said. "He does!"

The music played on, a driving beat followed by a pause. Bob started shouting "Cookie!" during the breaks. Lilith laughed and joined him. The pattern repeated, and the rest joined in.

They were having fun. It reminded Alex of his youth.

"Please don't do that at the club," Madison said. "I don't want them to think we're making fun of them."

They found an empty table next to the dance floor. Madison pulled out a twenty-dollar bill, waved it to get the waitress's attention, and ordered two pitchers of beer.

"I've got something for you," she said to Alex. She put something in his hand. "For your sensory issues."

It was a pair of earplugs.

"It's going to get loud," she said.

Alex smiled. He didn't deserve a girlfriend this perfect.

Two pitchers of beer arrived, with glasses for everyone.

"None for me," Alex said. He was the designated driver. He poured for everyone at the table.

Madison flagged down the waitress again. "Do you have any coffee? This guy's up past his bedtime." She pointed at Alex.

The waitress shook her head. "I'm sorry, no."

Madison produced another twenty. "Do you suppose you could make a fresh pot?"

"Sure, coming right up."

Madison knew how to get things done.

As the band took the stage, Alex asked, "Which one is Lars?"

"The guy on the right," Madison said.

She pointed to a tall, handsome guy with an electric guitar, long blond hair, and a sleeveless tunic that could have been bought at a medieval festival, showing off the defined muscles in his arms.

"He looks like Thor from the comic books," said Alex.

The group began to play, and Alex was happy to have the earplugs. Lilith, Bob, and Garth seemed to enjoy the music. Alex did, too, to be fair. But when the vocalist sang, Alex couldn't stop thinking of Cookie Monster.

Lars was a decent guitarist, or at least fast and flashy.

Near the end of the first set, Lars spotted Madison and locked eyes with her. It made Alex uncomfortable.

They wrapped up the set, and the vocalist said, "We'll be right back after a short break."

Lars set his guitar down and headed their way.

Madison stood and gave him a quick, obligatory hug.

"Thanks for coming out," said Lars. He stood back and looked Madison up and down. "You're looking good."

"Thanks," she said. "You, too."

"Yeah, working out, eating clean."

Madison introduced him to everyone, and they all fist-bumped him.

"Listen," Lars said to Madison, "we're playing in Grand Rapids tomorrow night. I was thinkin' you could ride along on the bus and hang out. I could drive you back home before work Monday."

"I can't. I'm seeing someone."

Alex was happy to hear her say that. Lars was disappointed but covered well. "That's cool. Moving on. I get it." He looked at Bob and Garth. "Is your new guy here? I'd like to meet him."

Madison put one arm around Alex's waist and a hand on his chest.

Lars was surprised. "You're with pops here?"

"Lars!"

Lars took a moment to size up Alex.

"Good for you," Lars said to Alex. "I hope I'm still a player when I'm your age." Lars slapped Alex on the back. "Well, I have to hit the can and rehydrate before the next set. It was good to meet all of you."

He headed for the dressing room.

"I'm sorry about that," Madison said to Alex. "See what I had to put up with?"

"It went like I expected."

They stayed for part of the next set, then Alex yawned despite the coffee.

"Okay, time to go," said Madison. She motioned to Lilith, Garth, and Bob.

Alex was moody on the way back to Ann Arbor.

"Lars hurt your feelings, didn't he?" Madison asked.

"It's not just that. He tried to get you to go to Grand Rapids with him."

"He just wanted a booty call. Maybe his groupies are jumping ship."

"And he got me thinking about our age difference."

"Come on. Women mature faster than men. I figure you and I are the same age, maturity-wise."

"There's no data to back that up," he said.

"It's only ten years. There have been plenty of couples with bigger age gaps."

"Like who?"

"Frank Sinatra and Mia Farrow."

"You see how well that worked out?"

"Mia Farrow and Woody Allen." She snickered. "Woody Allen and Soon-Yi Previn."

"You're sick," he said.

Their three passengers had gone quiet. She looked back.

"Aw," she said quietly.

"What's going on back there?"

"Lilith's got her head on Garth's shoulder, and she's holding Bob's hand." Madison sighed. "They're so cute when they're asleep."

Chapter 57

APARTMENT SHOPPING

One day, not long after, Madison paid a visit to Alex's office. He was staring at his computer monitor when she walked in.

"What are you doing?" she asked.

He looked up and smiled. She sat on his lap and kissed him.

"Looking for a place to live," he said.

"What are we thinking? Apartment? Condo? Mobile home?"

"I think I should start out small, at least until the dust settles from this divorce. I have to pay for Lucy's health insurance for eighteen months. I saw quotes that gave me a heart attack. Hannah starts college next fall. I'm hoping for scholarship money, but you never know."

"You could move in with me for a while," she said.

"Your place isn't big enough for *you*."

"We could get a place together, split the rent. Something bigger."

"That's going beyond casual, isn't it?"

"Too early?" she said.

"I think so ."

"I get it. You need your space." He couldn't tell if she was mocking him.

"Things are moving pretty fast," he said. "We've never actually dated."

"The Magic Stick," she said.

"If you go there with a carload of people from work, it's not a date."

"Seattle, then."

"That was work-related, too."

"Ok. You're right. But there's a simple solution."

"What did you have in mind?"

"Take me out somewhere," she said. "I'm not suggesting that we get serious. We can keep it casual. The sex is great, but I need more. You know what I see more than anything when we're together?"

"What?"

"The ceiling of my bedroom. It's getting old."

"Ok. Would you like to go out with me sometime?"

"I thought you'd never ask."

"What would you like to do?"

"Go apartment shopping."

He had to admire her persistence.

He made a list of apartments and condos that would suit him. Madison insisted on going with him to every showing. Her opinion was valuable, sometimes. Things like "There's not enough parking" or "The building's run-down." But she kept steering him towards the more spacious, more expensive choices—places big enough for two.

They looked at a luxury condo downtown. It was modern and beautiful, with plenty of room—the perfect location. It was affordable, but he balked.

"It's only a thousand square feet," he said.

"You've been looking at studios, for crying out loud!" Madison was exasperated.

"Yeah, but for this price, I'd expect more."

"You're driving me crazy!" she said.

The final showing for the day was a loft in a renovated building that had once been a factory. It had nice high ceilings but hardly any floor space.

"I like it," Alex said.

"It's small," said Madison. "It's another bachelor pad."

"So? I'm a bachelor."

Madison had had enough. "I'd like enough space for socks and underwear!"

"We agreed. I got married right out of college. I had obligations right away. Do you know what I see in the near future? Freedom. Total freedom. I've never had that before."

She stormed out into the hallway, and he followed. She beat him to the car. He was surprised to find her crying.

"You're the one that said, 'Let's keep it casual so nobody gets hurt,'" he said.

"You're right," she said. "I did say that. Casual it is." She wiped the tears from her eyes.

He tried to put his arms around her. She pushed him away and got into the car.

They were quiet on the way to her apartment. He was getting mixed messages from her. Being casual had been a good idea. It reduced the anxiety of being in a new relationship. He couldn't handle a serious commitment right now. He'd been through a lot recently, and as an introvert, his whole existence revolved around stress-reduction strategies.

She didn't know what she wanted. He could relate. So many variables and so many potential outcomes. Code was easy; people were hard.

He parked in front of her house.

"See you tomorrow," he said.

"Yeah." She gave him a quick kiss on the cheek and rushed away.

She typically invited him in when he took her home. He had the feeling that he had screwed up badly.

He stopped off at the liquor store on the way to his house.

When Alex got home, Lucy was making dinner.

"How was your day?" she asked.

He pulled a fifth of scotch out of a paper bag and twisted off the cap

"Just awesome," he said.

"Did something happen at work?" she asked.

He got a whiskey glass out of the cabinet.

"I don't want to talk about it," he said and went to the basement.

He turned on the stereo, put in a Metallica cd, and cranked up the volume. He filled the whiskey glass with scotch and sat in the recliner.

He drank and brooded until it was time for bed.

Chapter 58

NOVEMBER: THE CHILL SETS IN

Madison passed his office when she got in. She usually stopped to chat and give him a kiss on the way to her office. Not today.

He gave her a few minutes to settle in before visiting her.

He knocked on her door jamb. She looked up.

"Good morning," she said. It wasn't the warm greeting she usually gave him. She was still pissed.

"I'm sorry," he said.

"For what?"

"For hurting your feelings."

She shrugged without saying anything.

"Are you free Saturday night?" he asked. "Maybe we could catch a movie."

She hesitated. "I need time alone."

"I understand." Alone time was important to him, too, but he was surprised to hear her say it. They'd been practically joined at the hip since Seattle, and he wasn't exactly holding her hostage.

"Anything else?" she asked him. Perfunctory.

"About Thanksgiving—do you have any plans?"

"I'm probably going to Wisconsin."

"You're welcome at our house."

"*Your house,* meaning yours and Lucy's." She took a breath. "I don't think so. I don't want things to be awkward."

"I ran it by Lucy. She's fine with it."

"I wasn't talking about Lucy." She drew in a breath. "I should spend time with my family, and you should spend time with yours."

Did she mean that to be hurtful? If she did, she succeeded. Spending a holiday separately with their families would be natural under different circumstances. But now it was official—he was screwed.

He returned to his office, reflecting that his life was just one hot mess after another.

Chapter 59

GOODBYE, OLD MAN

One night in early November, Lucy was having trouble falling asleep. Kay had been over, but neither had felt like making love. They talked for a while, then Kay went home to sleep with her husband.

After midnight, Lucy saw flashing lights coming through the bedroom window and reflecting off the wall. She was fully awake now and looked outside.

An ambulance was below, in the Holloways' crescent driveway.

Lucy ran down the stairs, put on slippers and a winter coat, and ran next door.

EMTs hauled Frank's body out on a gurney, face covered. Kay stood by the ambulance, crying and shivering, in a nightgown. Lucy opened her coat and pulled Kay into her.

"He's gone," Kay sobbed. "His heart..."

Lucy pulled her in tighter and kissed the top of her head.

Alex approached them.

"Frank?" he asked.

"Yeah," Lucy said.

Out of character, Alex came close and hugged them both.

"I'll stay with you tonight," Lucy said to Kay. "I'll help you take care of things in the morning." She guided Kay to the front door.

Frank's death wasn't a surprise. He'd known his time was short. The surprise was that a heart attack killed him, not the cancer. But he had been fond of his red meat.

At the cemetery, Lucy wondered if anything could be as gloomy as a November funeral in Michigan. She was surprised at the turn-out, both at the church and at the graveside. The Holloways had been in town for only half a year, but the church had filled, the procession was long, and many cars were parked along the snaking drive of the cemetery. They were mostly older couples, Frank's age.

"People from the country club," Kay said. "He was a lousy golfer, but everybody loved him."

"He was a good guy," Lucy said.

"I'm going to miss that old man."

Lucy tried to pick out Frank's ex-wife and children in the crowd, but Kay told her that they didn't show. They all had "prior engagements."

Alex looked on from a distance, and she waved. He nodded in acknowledgment.

"They're selling the house," Kay said.

Lucy's heart sank. "Why?"

"The attorney for Frank's estate contacted me. Almost everything goes to Frank's three kids. He left me the condo in Maui and a trust fund. I guess I'm moving."

"When?"

"The sooner, the better. This weather's starting to get to me." She looked Lucy in the eyes.

"Stay," Lucy said. "We can find a place together."

"Frank has moved on. You're on solid ground. My next adventure is in Maui. The Fates have decided."

Kay made it sound set in stone. Lucy let it go. Now was not the time to argue with a grieving widow.

They kissed, said goodbye, and drove home in separate cars.

Lucy thought about Kay until bedtime, expecting to cry, but she never did.

Things change, she told herself. *You have to adapt.*

Chapter 60

CHARTS AND SPREADSHEETS

Alex had to think about the whole "casual" thing. Madison didn't seem to know what she wanted. Neither did he. Someone had to make a decision. He did what he typically did in similar situations: he started a flowchart of actions and consequences, and a spreadsheet of pros and cons.

The flowchart got complicated quickly—too many variables. He abandoned it temporarily and focused on the list of pros and cons. Things like:

Madison was beautiful. That went into the pro column.

Madison was really good at sex. That also went into the pro column.

There was a significant age difference. Con.

He enjoyed being with Madison. Pro.

If they got serious only to break up, which was sure to happen, it was really going to hurt, even worse than he was hurting now. Con.

Madison was one of the most intelligent people he'd ever met. Pro.

A serious relationship would mean giving up a lot of freedom. Con.

He was sure she could do better than him, another reason it wouldn't last. Con.

Madison obviously still had a connection with Lars, as much as she denied it. The guy looked like a comic book superhero. It would be hard to compete with that. Yet another reason it wouldn't last. Con

She looked like Kathleen Sears, but he wasn't sure sex fantasy data warranted being on the list of parameters.

That made the whole process suspect. Not all the data carried equal weight. If he took the time to weigh the data, that would add whole layers of complexity.

He took a break from the process. It was giving him a headache.

Fuck it, he told himself.

He stopped drinking until he was sober enough to drive. He went to the mall to shop for something expensive.

It would either be great or the worst mistake of his life.

Chapter 61

ALEX TRIES TO COMMUNICATE

Alex was desperate to talk to Madison. There never seemed to be a good time. Madison was making sure of it. It was usually hard for him to share his feelings, but it became impossible when the other party wasn't willing to listen.

The week before Thanksgiving, he tried to talk to her several times at work. She kept saying, "Not now, I'm busy," or "I don't want to have this discussion at work." But when he tried to see her outside work, she would say, "Not tonight. I don't feel up to it."

One time she said, "We do need to talk. I'll see you after Thanksgiving."

That suited Alex. Now he had time to practice what he would say and reduce the chances of screwing it up.

Madison told him she was flying to Wisconsin the Saturday before Thanksgiving. She didn't have any sales meetings coming up, and she could use the extra time off.

"Can I see you before you go?" he asked.

"No," she said.

Chapter 62
THANKSGIVING

The kitchen smelled festive, of dressing and sage, of pumpkin, cinnamon, and ginger. Alex sat at the breakfast nook with a double scotch on the rocks, staring at the wall. Lucy opened the oven door and pulled out the turkey. The doorbell rang.

"Alex, could you get that?" Lucy asked.

"Sure," he said.

He opened the front door to find Kay bearing bags of groceries and a casserole.

"Come on in," he said, reaching out to relieve her of some of her load. She hugged him. He followed her to the kitchen. "Are you doing okay?" he asked.

"Yeah. It wasn't a surprise. We knew he didn't have much time left."

She hugged Hannah, then kissed Lucy. The three women set the table while Alex nursed his drink and stayed out of their way.

When everything was ready, the four sat at the table. Alex brought his bottle of scotch.

Lucy said, "Our family tradition is to hold hands and say what we're thankful for."

"I like that," Kay said.

They all joined hands.

"Hannah, you first."

"I'm thankful for my mom and dad. And I'm thankful that I got accepted at Stanford."

"And I'm thankful for the scholarship money that allows my brilliant daughter to go to Stanford," said Lucy. "And I'm thankful that I'm getting to know myself. Kay?"

"I'm grateful to all of you for helping me get through this," Kay said. "And I'm thankful Alex doesn't hate my guts anymore."

"Well... you're not so bad," Alex said.

There was a long pause.

"Your turn, Alex," Lucy said. "What are you thankful for?"

He earnestly tried to think of something. He came up empty.

"I'm not hungry," he said as he stood. "I've got work to do." He took his bottle of scotch with him to the basement.

The three women ate for a while in silence. Kay didn't know what to think.

"It's not me, is it?" Kay asked.

"No," Lucy said.

"I thought he didn't drink."

"That was the old Alex," said Lucy. "The new Alex drinks like a fish."

"What happened?" Kay asked.

Lucy looked at Hannah. "Could you excuse us for a few minutes? I need to speak with Kay."

Hannah was indignant. "I should be in on this conversation."

"Hannah's right," Kay said. "Let her stay. If it affects you, it affects her."

"Fine," Lucy replied. "Things went south with Rebound Girl."

"The poor guy," said Kay. "He's miserable. What are we going to do?"

"We?" Lucy asked.

"If it affects you, it affects me. We're all in this together."

Chapter 63

BLACK FRIDAY

Alex was plagued by a headache and a queasy stomach when he woke. He went upstairs, where a pot of coffee waited for him in the kitchen. He drank two cups before he started work. He needed to rehydrate, but he also needed the caffeine. He rummaged through the Thanksgiving leftovers. There were plenty. He ate enough to settle his unruly gut.

When he got the computer running, he found he couldn't focus. And to top it off, the headache got worse. He decided he might as well add scotch to the coffee, which helped the headache but hindered the concentration.

He occasionally heard footsteps and muffled conversation from upstairs.

Sometime around late afternoon, Lucy opened the door to the basement.

"You okay down there?" she called.

"Yeah, I'm fine," he lied.

"Okay. Just checking," she said. "There's more coffee if you need it."

"Thanks."

He knew he should try to make contact, to show his appreciation for Lucy's attempt to have a normal Thanksgiving, but his mood was so bad that he didn't feel like subjecting anyone else to it.

The headache came back. He opened the top drawer of his desk, hoping to find a bottle of ibuprofen. Instead, he found the bottle of Percocet that his doctor had prescribed before his back surgery. He had stopped taking them after Madison told him about Lars and his substance abuse problem.

He took a pill and chased it with scotch. He waited a while for the headache to go away. When it didn't, he took another. It wasn't helping.

Nothing was helping.

He looked at the bottle. He had been prescribed forty of them. He figured he had about thirty left.

"Fuck it," he said. He held the bottle up and emptied it into his mouth. He took a long swig from the bottle of scotch and staggered to the recliner.

There, he said, *that should do it.*

He didn't have any idea what a fatal dose of Percocet was. He didn't really care. If he died, he died.

A warm fog enveloped his mind, and he drifted off into oblivion. He heard the sound of ocean waves crashing on a beach.

"Alex!" someone said. "What have you done?"

"Kay?"

"Get up, get up!" She pulled him to his feet. "Come, you must purge!"

She led him to the bathroom and set him in front of the toilet. He vomited right away as she stroked his back.

"Why would you do this?" A soft blue glow surrounded her.

He stopped retching. "Everything's turned to shit," he said.

"Not everything. There is some shit, for sure, but you have people who love you," she said. "Lucy, Hannah, and the one who ran away. And me. We all love you. You can't do this to us." She cradled his head. "It's okay to cry," she said.

So he cried, for the first time since fourth grade.

He tried to look at her, but his eyes wouldn't focus. All he could see was the blue glow.

"Now is not your time. You have important things to do," she said. "We will try to fix this. Until then, no more silly games. Be strong. Promise me."

"Okay...okay..."

He wiped his mouth and stood.

"Kay?"

She was gone—if she had ever really been there at all.

Chapter 64

WHERE IN THE WORLD IS MADISON LUNDQUIST?

The following Monday, the staff entered the conference room for the daily meeting.

Alex looked as bad as he felt. He hadn't slept well. He hadn't shaved or bathed in a few days. It wasn't worth the effort.

Madison wasn't returning phone calls or texts.

Brad called the meeting to order and was interrupted by Lilith.

"Where's Madison?" she asked.

"You two are pretty close," Brad said. "You don't know what's going on?"

"The last I heard, she was supposed to be back today," Lilith said. "I guess we're not as close as I thought."

"Maybe Alex knows something," Brad said.

When all eyes turned to Alex, he shrugged and shook his head. That was his last day in the office. After that, he started working from home.

Lucy was worried. Something had to be done. No one in the world knew her husband as well as she and Brad. Maybe if they put their heads together, they could come up with a plan. She went to see Brad.

They sat in the break room talking over coffee.

"Did you know we were splitting up?" Lucy asked him.

"Yeah, I saw that coming," Brad said.

"Did Alex tell you why?"

"Yeah. Didn't see *that* coming."

"Neither did I, believe it or not." Lucy sighed. "We couldn't give each other what we needed."

"This thing with Madison worried me," Brad said. "You can't date the people you work with. It never works out."

"The heart wants what it wants."

"My heart wants a smooth-running organization. This is crippling us."

Brad filled her in on the things Alex hadn't told her. Everything had been going fine—all lovey-dovey with public displays of affection. Toward the end of October, the new lovers stopped talking to each other unless it was work-related. Everyone at Tucker-Herman had noticed. Alex wouldn't talk about it.

"How's his work been?" Lucy asked.

"Solid. He's sharper when he's drunk than most people are when they're sober," Brad said. "Madison is the one that's hurting us. She had been pulling a lot of weight with the smaller clients, and now she's gone."

"She quit?"

Brad shrugged. "Leave of absence, technically. She took off early for Thanksgiving. She called me Friday and said she didn't know when she'd be back, or even *if* she'd be back. She had to get her head together, she said. Her phone goes straight to voicemail."

"What a mess."

"Alex needs a therapist."

"Can't get him to go. If he keeps on this way, he'll need a rehab clinic. What the hell happened? I saw them at the picnic."

"He said it was a joke, trying to get under my skin."

"I know what I saw. I probably knew what was going on before he did."

"What do we do now?" Brad asked. It was unsettling. Brad was usually the guy with the solutions.

"What kind of person is Madison?" Lucy asked him.

"She's a good employee. She's indispensable."

"I mean, is she a good person? I put Alex through a lot. I don't want him to get hurt again."

"Yeah. She's good people."

"Then there's only one thing to do—find her and bring her back."

"Easier said than done."

"We've got to try. You've got some talented people working for you. Is there a way to find someone using the internet?" Lucy asked.

He smiled at her naivete. "You're kidding, right?"

"Yes? No? What are you trying to say?"

"There are a million ways to track a person on the internet. But it's called cyber-stalking."

Lucy was disappointed.

Brad stood. "Still," he said. "Follow me. Maybe we can recruit some volunteers."

He led Lucy down the hall to the pit. A cacophony came from beyond the door. It sounded like a war was going on, a loud multiplayer game. He opened the door and stepped inside.

"Glad to see the crew hard at work," he shouted over the noise.

Garth said, "Oh, shit!" as he removed his headphones. The rest of the staff stopped their play, removed their gear, and gave him their full attention.

"We have a visitor," Brad said. "She'd like to have a few words with you." He motioned Lucy into the room.

She was apologetic.

"Does everyone know who I am?" Lucy asked.

Lilith spoke. "You're Alex's wife."

"Call me Lucy."

"How's he doing?" asked Garth.

"Not good."

"Madison..." said Lilith, then she covered her mouth as if she'd spilled a secret.

"Yes, Madison. Don't worry. Everybody knows."

"I bet you're pissed," said Bob.

"No. I'm the one who screwed things up. I won't blame anyone but myself. I care a lot about Alex. I want him to be happy. Even if it's with someone else."

"It's called compersion," said Lilith.

Lucy nodded, surprised that there was a word for it.

"What do you want from us?" asked Garth.

"Alex has been a total wreck since Madison left. I was wondering if you could help me find her."

"Why?"

"So I can bring her back."

"There's an ethical dilemma here," Garth said.

"I know, cyberstalking. I'll take responsibility. I'll sign a waiver if I have to."

Brad clapped his hands. "Okay, you're all witnesses. If this ends up in court, it's on her." Everyone nodded. "Okay, crew! New assignment: find Madison Lundquist!"

He expected enthusiasm, but Garth said, "We're kind of busy."

"Bullshit! I just heard World of Warcraft or whatever thundering through this steel door a few minutes ago."

"Bob's doing beta-testing for Media-Lab, and we all decided to help him out."

"What I'm hearing is that you need an incentive. Okay. The first person to give me a good address gets a one-week all-expenses paid trip to..."

"Cancun!" shouted Lilith.

"Cancun it is," said Brad.

They all swiveled in their chairs. Everyone in the room started the search, keyboards clacking. Lilith stroked a crystal that hung from her neck. Things went on like this for a long time. Lucy paced the room.

"Wait," said Bob. "There is no Madison Lundquist."

"What?" Brad said.

"She doesn't exist."

"What database did you plug into?" asked Lilith.

"Zaba."

"Amateur!"

Lucy was puzzled. "Did you do a background check before you hired her?" she asked Brad.

Brad shrugged. "Her interview was impressive. I would have hired her even if her CV was phony." Which it now appeared to be.

This kind of activity was out of Lucy's wheelhouse. She helped by providing coffee and taking fast food orders.

After a couple of hours, Lilith cried out, "I got a hit!"

Garth and Bob stood to get a look at her monitor. She stood and shielded it from their prying eyes.

"Back off!" she growled. "I need a vacation!"

It occurred to Brad that they *all* could use a vacation. This needed to be a team effort, not an individual competition. "Okay, I'm changing the rules. I want you to share your information. Find Madison, and *everyone* gets a vacation."

It took them twenty-two minutes after that.

They had to work backward. This was the information trail that led them to Madison's place of refuge:

The Facebook page of Lars's death metal group, Grand Maul; there were no friends or fans with the name Madison Lundquist, but there was a Madison Bennet—the bad photograph looked like it could be her.

A recorded marriage license in Los Angeles confirmed it.

A name-change document told them that Madison Bennet had previously been Mary Jo Kowalski, born in Milwaukee, who had resided in Eau Claire, Wisconsin, and had shared a house with a Colleen Kowalski Schmidt. Colleen was still living at the address, according to several databases.

If Madison had gone to Wisconsin to visit family for Thanksgiving, the odds were that it would be there.

Lilith wrote the address on a sticky note and gave it to Lucy.

"Good hunting, sister," Lilith said.

Chapter 65

ODYSSEY

When Lucy got home, she asked Hannah if she was up for a road trip.

"Yes, I am so bored. Where?"

"Eau Claire, Wisconsin."

"Okay. Why?"

"We're going to find your father's girlfriend and bring her back." She was that confident.

"We're not using ropes and duct tape, are we?"

"No, sweetie, we'll use good, old-fashioned persuasion." Whatever that might entail. Lucy didn't know what she'd say when she got there. She'd have time to figure it out on the road.

They packed their bags that night. They didn't need much. If things went well, this would be just a two-day trip.

Early the following day, Lucy went to the basement to check on Alex. He was in bed, covered by the blankets, except for his feet. The basement smelled like pizza, scotch, and dirty socks.

"Hannah and I are going on a trip. We should be back tomorrow night."

"Drive safe," he mumbled. "Love you."

"Love you, too."

She saw something unusual on the corner of his computer desk—a small velvet box. She picked it up and opened it. It held a beautiful ring with an impressive diamond.

"You dog," she said.

She closed the box, put it in her coat pocket, and headed to the SUV.

When she got there, Kay was putting a bag into the back.

"Thanks for asking me to come along," Kay said.

"You could use a distraction," Lucy said. "Thanks for coming." Kay would be leaving soon. Every minute with her was precious.

Hannah was in the back with a sack of snacks and a small cooler filled with beverages.

"Eau Claire, Wisconsin," Kay said. "How long is this going to take?"

"Roughly eight and a half hours," Hannah said. "Not counting pit stops."

"We should get there by six pm if the roads aren't too bad."

Lucy pulled the velvet box out of her coat and opened it for Kay and Hannah to see.

"Look at that rock!" Kay said.

"He was going to propose, but she flew the coop," Lucy said.

Lucy steered the car onto the street.

She thought about the ring. It irritated her for two reasons:

Number one—her engagement ring looked like it had come out of a bubblegum machine. She and Alex had gotten married in leaner times, but still...

Number two—Alex was always dragging his feet about everything, a perpetual victim of decision paralysis. Who knows how long he'd had the ring? Maybe he could have avoided all this drama if he'd manned up and popped the question in a timely manner.

Well. What was done was done. She didn't have time or inclination to ruminate. The only thing to do now was try to fix it. She was on a mission.

The road trip was a good idea. Hannah and Kay got a chance to become acquainted. They seemed to like each other, and that made Lucy happy. As Kay said, life's good when the people you love can love each other.

They hit a traffic jam just before Chicago and a snowstorm north of it. It was dark and cold when Lucy parked the SUV in front of the house.

"You have arrived," said the voice from the phone's navigation.

Lucy compared the number on the piece of paper with the number on the house once more. Lights were on in the living room. Someone was home.

"Well, here goes," said Lucy. "If she's here, I'll give you a thumbs-up."

Kay opened her door. "I have to get out and stretch. My ass is numb."

Lucy walked up to the front door and knocked. Footsteps approached. The door was opened by a stout woman in her forties.

"Yes?" said the woman.

"Is there a Madison Lundquist here?"

The color drained from the woman's face. She closed the door. There were voices. The door opened again.

"Who should I say is calling?" the woman asked.

"Lucy Herman."

The woman closed the door again.

"How did she find me?" said Madison from inside. Lucy turned and gave the thumbs-up.

"I don't know! What do we do?" asked the stout woman.

"I don't know!"

"Let's see what she's got to say."

"Don't..."

The door opened again.

"Won't you come in?" the woman said.

Lucy walked in timidly.

"Can I take your coat?"

"I don't know how long I'll be staying."

Madison was on the sofa, glaring at the other woman. "Lucy, this is my sister, Colleen," Madison said.

"Nice to meet you," Lucy said.

"So, what brings you to Wisconsin?" Madison asked.

"I came to take you back."

"You can't be serious."

There was a knock on the door. Colleen opened it. Kay was there, shivering. "Can I use your bathroom? I can't hold it any longer."

"Sure," Colleen said, pointing. "Right down the hall."

Hannah came in as well. "Me, too."

"My friend Kay, my daughter Hannah," said Lucy.

"I've met Hannah," Madison said.

Lucy looked at Madison again. "We need you to come back."

"We, who?"

"Everyone, especially Alex. He's miserable without you. Why did you leave?"

"I needed time to clear my head."

"About what? He can be a handful, but you probably knew that before Seattle."

Madison stood and turned to the side. She lifted her sweatshirt to reveal a bulge that didn't come from beer and pretzels—a baby bump.

The tarot reading. Big change. The birth of a child. It was all coming true.

"Oh, my! How far along are you?"

"Three months."

"Alex is the father?"

"Of course," Madison said. "What kind of girl do you think I am?"

"You haven't told him?"

Madison sat again and shook her head. "He made it pretty clear he didn't want to be tied down."

Lucy laughed.

"He doesn't know what he wants. He's going to be over the moon when he finds out."

Kay returned to the living room.

"What's going on?" she asked.

"Madison's pregnant."

"Are we happy or sad?" Kay asked.

"Trying to figure that out," Madison said. "I'm going through with it. That's all I know."

Hannah came back into the room.

"Hannah," Lucy said, "you're going to be a big sister."

"Are you kidding me?"

Lucy remembered the felt box in her coat pocket. She pulled it out and showed it to Madison.

"What's that?" Madison asked.

"A little gift from Alex."

Lucy opened the box.

A whimsy overtook her. She got down on one knee and said, "Madison Lundquist, will you marry my husband?"

Madison smirked. "This is kind of sudden. Could I have some time to think about it?"

Lucy stood again. "Of course. But at least come back and talk to him. This is big. He needs to hear it from you, in person."

"You're right," Madison said. "But..." Her voice drifted off.

"But what?"

"He still loves you."

"Well, sure. We've been married for over twenty years. You can't just turn it off like a light switch." Lucy took a breath. "I owe you an apology."

"For what?"

"I thought you were just the rebound girl. But this is real."

Madison looked at her without speaking.

Lucy continued. "It's your time now. We broke the eggs. Let's see if we can make a good quiche."

Madison said. "I'll come back."

"Great," said Lucy.

"I'm not promising anything."

"Understood," Lucy said. She looked at Colleen. "We need a place to spend the night. Any good hotels around here?"

"There's a bunch of hotels," Colleen said. "But none of them make the kind of breakfast I make on a Sunday morning. You're welcome to stay right here."

"I don't want to inconvenience you."

"Nonsense. We have plenty of room if the youngster's okay with the couch."

Kay pointed at herself and Lucy. "We'll sleep together," Kay said. "We're a couple."

Colleen tried not to show her surprise. “Even better. Hannah can have a bed to herself. Well, make yourselves comfortable. Let me take your coats. Casablanca’s on the tube in a few minutes. I’m making popcorn. Does anybody want a beer?”

The following day, Lucy woke to the smell of coffee, sausages, and biscuits. Colleen was right. The breakfast she made put the chain hotels to shame.

When breakfast was over and the dishes put away, the travelers formed a line on the walk with their bags.

“I’m up for a baby shower,” Colleen said. “I’ve never been east of Chicago.”

“There’ll be a baby shower,” Lucy said. “I’ll make sure of it.”

Colleen hugged Lucy. “You look after my little sister,” she said.

“I will.”

Colleen hugged Hannah. “You take care, missy. Good luck with college and all that.”

Colleen hugged Kay. “I’m glad I got to meet you,” she said.

And finally, Madison. “You’ve got an interesting situation here,” Colleen said. “I hope it works out. But I’m just a phone call away if you need anything.”

“I love you, sis,” said Madison. “I’ll talk to you soon.”

Chapter 66

RETURN TO ITHACA

"Shotgun!" said Kay as they headed for the car.

"No," Lucy said. "Madison sits in front with me. We need to talk." Lucy had advice that she wanted to share.

Things like:

"You probably know this already, but Alex doesn't like to be touched unless he's comfortable with you."

Madison confirmed that she had found that out, but they were well past that obstacle.

"He's got a database for everything—car maintenance, furnace inspections, medical exams. And they're all integrated with Google Calendar. If you get an oil change, you have to let him know so he can enter the data."

"I can live with that," Madison said.

Lucy laughed. "Yeah, it's not so bad."

"He has deep feelings. He just isn't good at showing them." Madison had discovered that, too.

"He likes dinner at 6:30. Heavy on vegetables, light on red meat and saturated fat."

"That might be a problem. I'm not much of a cook," said Madison.

"That's okay. I can teach you."

Madison wasn't sure she wanted to learn or perform a homemaker's traditional duties. Lucy kept saying *we* as if Alex's happiness was a project they'd collaborate on, the soon-to-be ex-wife and the potential future wife. Lucy was grooming Madison to be her replacement in the marriage. It was strange.

They stopped a few times for bathroom breaks and to refuel. They switched drivers east of Gary, Indiana, with Kay behind the wheel and Lucy and Madison in the back.

The mentoring continued.

"Alex needs plenty of alone time."

"Sometimes, when he's quiet, he'll have an expression on his face like he's angry. He hardly ever gets angry, though. He's probably just working out a problem in his head."

Madison had seen that look. It had worried her until she figured it out, then she found this intensity attractive.

"One more thing," Lucy said. "He's been drinking a lot." That was disturbing. "Don't worry," Lucy continued. "He's not too far gone. I think we can fix it."

Madison hoped so. She wasn't going to raise a child with an alcoholic or any other type of substance abuser. She had learned her lesson with Lars.

"Have you had an ultrasound yet?" Lucy asked.

"Last week," Madison replied.

"And?"

"Everything looked good."

"I meant— boy or girl?"

"It's too early to be sure, but we think we spotted a baby penis."

Lucy smiled. "When Hannah was three, Alex asked her what she wanted for Christmas. She said a baby brother. It was sad because that was all she asked for that year, and I couldn't have any more kids." She looked at Hannah. "It may take your father a while, but he always comes through."

"You seem like a smart girl," Lucy said, "I'm not being judgemental, I swear. How did you end up getting pregnant?"

Madison had asked herself the same question hundreds of times over the last few months. There were several reasons:

She'd bought a package of condoms for the trip to Seattle, thinking something romantic might happen, without any evidence. She'd left the condoms on the table by the apartment door, sure that nothing would happen, and ashamed of herself for hoping.

That little voice in her head, the biological clock that said it was time to have a child before it was too late. She'd been hearing the voice over the last couple of years, getting louder and more frequent. At least she'd been wise enough to make Lars use condoms. Getting pregnant with him would have been a disaster.

The fact that her period had just ended a day before Seattle. She would have bet her life that she wasn't ovulating.

Madison looked down at her lap.

"I don't know," she said. That was the simple, honest answer. She looked at Lucy. "I'm not sorry."

"Neither am I." Lucy put her hand on Madison's.

When they got to Ann Arbor, Madison wanted to go to her apartment to freshen up.

"No, he needs you now," Lucy said.

When they arrived at the Herman home, Lucy led Madison to the basement.

"Alex," Lucy said. "You have a visitor."

"Go away," he said.

"He's *your* problem now," Lucy said, and she went up the stairs.

"Alex," Madison said. "I've got some news."

"Madison? Is that you?"

She got into bed with him and sniffed the air. "When was the last time you bathed?"

"It's been a while."

Lucy got ready for bed. The mission had been successful, but it had been a long, crazy weekend.

She cried a little as she fell asleep.

Chapter 67

BALM

When Alex woke the next day, he wandered upstairs. Lucy and Madison were in the kitchen.

"Madison," he said.

She looked at him and smiled. "Good morning. Lucy's teaching me how to make quiche," she said. "Let's take a break," she said to Lucy. "I'd like to go for a walk," she said to Alex.

Alex and Madison donned the boots and coats waiting by the front door. It was cold outside.

She led him to the playground nearby. When they got there, she offered a hand for him to hold. She pulled him to the swings. She sat on one, and he sat next to her.

"Do you remember what I said last night?" she asked.

"We're having a baby."

"How do you feel about that?"

"Good." She frowned at him. "I mean, really good," he corrected. "Fantastic. I can't wait."

"You mean it? Lucy vouched for you. She said you're a good father."

He nodded again.

"Kind of puts a crimp in your 'total freedom' idea, doesn't it?"

"Well...that was just some big talk. I wanted a pony when I was five, but I got over it." He frowned. "I'm sorry. My head hurts. My stomach's a mess. Hangover."

"Yeah, about that," she said. "I hear you've been drinking a lot. Is that going to be a problem?"

"I'll quit. I'll get help if I have to."

"You swear? Your son needs a sober father."

"I swear. I don't even like alcohol. But it helped with..." He stopped.

"The pain?" She finished what he couldn't say.

He nodded.

"Why were you in pain?" she asked.

"I guess... because I love you so much." He had thought those words many times, but that was the first time he had said them out loud.

"Ah, there we go. Well then, I guess I love you, too." She smiled. "Made you say it first. I win." She laughed. Her laughter was like the balm of a healer.

"Thanks for giving me another chance," he said.

"Right back at you, mister. One more thing."

"Yeah?"

She took a velvet box from her coat and handed it to him.

"Your wife had to propose to me. Does that seem right to you?"

He stammered for a second.

"I thought I'd wait until the divorce was final," he said.

"You think too much. You left me hanging."

"After I bought the ring, you kept putting me off. Then you left and stopped answering your phone."

"Okay, we're both idiots. But now's your chance to fix it."

Alex stood. He got down on one knee. He opened the box.

"Madison Lundquist, will you marry me?"

"Of course, I'll marry you."

He put the ring on her finger, and she kissed him. She backed the swing up.

"Now look out," she said.

He retreated to a safe distance, and she began to swing.

Chapter 68

WHEN THE STUDENT IS TRULY READY, THE TEACHER DISAPPEARS

The estate attorney sold Frank's furniture at auction. His clothes and golf clubs were donated to The Salvation Army. That was fine with Kay. She didn't want anything. She had memories. She'd start over, and Maui was the best place she could think of to begin again.

The Holloway home sold two days after it was listed. Frank's children would be happy—it was a hot real estate market, and the house fetched a good price.

Kay stayed with the Hermans while the estate business was being settled. Lucy savored every minute of her company. But eventually, it was time for Kay to leave.

Lucy took Kay to the airport on Kay's last day. They talked about Lucy's husband proposing to his mistress as they walked to the security queue.

"I wish I could have been there," Kay said. "I love a good proposal."

"Alex needed his privacy," Lucy said. "Besides, you were there for the practice run." They stopped. Lucy wrapped Kay up in a bear hug, then released her. "Safe travels, girlfriend," she said.

"You know, you could come to Maui," Kay said. "You'd love it! Just get on the next flight."

"I can't do that. My life is here."

"I knew you'd say that, but I had to ask. Love is complicated, isn't it? No one knows that better than me. I want you to promise me something—start dating again."

"Maybe. Someday."

"Don't wait too long. Life is short."

"I promise."

"Visit when you get the chance. Bring the whole family. I can't wait to meet the baby. Auntie Kay will teach him how to surf." Lucy laughed again as tears filled her eyes.

A sunbeam came down and bathed Kay in light. She turned slowly, taking it all in one last time. She faced Lucy again and looked at her in adoration.

"The fates led me to you for a reason," Kay said. "This story was never about you loving me. This was about you loving yourself."

She turned and entered the security line.

Lucy watched her snake through the queue with her carry-on, to the TSA agent who checked her ID and boarding pass, to the conveyor where she emptied her pockets and took off her shoes. She held up her arms at the scanner and exited the other side. She turned and smiled at Lucy.

She blew a kiss, waved, then, poof! She was gone.

Chapter 69
RESOLUTION

Alex and Lucy talked to the realtor that sold the Holloways' home. She gave them an appraisal based on the square footage of the house, its condition, and the values of similar houses in the neighborhood. She sat with them in the family room as she crunched the numbers.

"There," she said. "That's the total." She handed the clipboard to Alex. His eyes got wide.

"Holy cow!" he said. It had been twenty years, and houses in that neighborhood had substantially increased in value.

Alex handed the clipboard to Lucy. "You're getting half of that," Alex said. "I think you're going to be okay."

Lucy wasn't so sure. The amount was impressive, but there were more important things than money.

"Talk it over," the realtor said. "I'll be back in a few days with the sales agreement."

There was nothing to talk about.

Lucy found a small apartment with a short-term lease that would be her temporary home until the money from the divorce settlement came through. She and Hannah would live together until Hannah went off to college. Alex would stay with Madison until they could find a larger apartment.

They bought moving boxes and started packing.

The realtor came back a few days later. She stuck a for sale sign into the front lawn and made rounds of the house, making notes on a clipboard. A photographer took pictures. Soon the house would be listed on the internet. Strangers would use Alex's technology to view the home like predatory birds eyeing prey.

The realtor was in the kitchen when her phone rang.

"Yes, I'm at the property. Next door to the last one. The commission will be 70k if I don't have to split." She sounded happy.

Alex, Lucy, Madison, and Hannah were packing things—pictures, knick-knacks, and the many other things that made a house a home. Alex's Landy award was now missing from the mantle, in a box somewhere.

Lucy's eyes were getting moist. She told herself to hold it together. But everything was disappearing, being put into boxes. She had no idea where anything would end up. It felt as though *she* was disappearing, too. It was all so uncertain. She had put her soul into this house. She whimpered and caught herself. She tried to stop it, but something in her broke. She sat on the sofa and bawled. Hannah sat on one side and put her arm around her. Madison sat, too. Lucy sobbed into Madison's shoulder.

"It's too much," Lucy said. "I just can't..."

"What's wrong?" asked Alex. "I thought you were okay with everything."

"Are you kidding me? I lost you, I lost Kay, and now I'm losing my house. I love this house."

Madison patted her back. "I do, too."

Alex was sympathetic, but he was at a loss. "We have to do this. We have to move forward."

"Why?" Madison asked.

"Because that's what people do."

"What people?"

"Everybody." He was perturbed. They had to sell the house to satisfy the terms of the divorce. Madison, of all people, should be with him on this. He couldn't understand why she was being difficult. Both women were being difficult.

"We could keep the house," Hannah said.

"You know, we could," said Madison. All *three* of them now. "It's a big house. There's room for all of us."

"You think?" said Lucy.

"I don't see why not."

"That's ridiculous," said Alex. "We can't get married unless I get divorced."

"I don't care," said Madison.

"What?"

"I don't care," she repeated. "I've got you, I've got the ring—I don't need a piece of paper."

"But—"

"—It'll be nice to have a baby in the house again," Lucy said.

"We can raise him together," Madison said.

"Yes!" said Lucy, wiping her eyes with a shirt sleeve. "We can make this work!"

"Hey!" Alex raised his voice to get their attention. They looked his way. "Do I get a vote?" he asked.

"Of course, you get a vote," Madison said. "On the question of keeping the house—all in favor say 'aye.'"

Lucy, Madison, and Hannah all said, "Aye."

"All opposed?"

They gave Alex a defiant look.

"The 'ayes' have it," said Madison.

The women hugged. Lucy cried tears of joy now. Madison waved him over. "Come here, you!"

He joined the huddle. He looked up at the ceiling as if to say, "Do you see what's going on down here?" If there were gods up there, surely they were having a good laugh.

"Okay," he said. "Okay."

He surrendered. Then he laughed himself, loudly, from his soul. He'd never laughed like that before in his life. What an incredible joke! It was all so crazy!

His life had never been normal. *He* had never been normal. Why start now?

He saw the realtor lurking at the edge of the room. She had witnessed the whole exchange. They still hadn't signed the sales agreement.

"Sorry," Alex said to her. "We've changed our minds."

The realtor's face turned red.

"Well, damnit!" she said.

Chapter 70

A NEW BEGINNING

Alex and Lucy withdrew their divorce petition. Divorce was still a possibility somewhere down the road, but for now, everyone was happy with how things were.

It wasn't a traditional household, but as Madison said once, "Tradition is just peer pressure from dead people."

Alex joined Alcoholics Anonymous. He wasn't sure he needed to, but he was the kind of guy who liked to err on the side of caution. He found it to be a fine institution and made some good friends there.

Madison changed her last name again. Alex and Lucy's last names were "Herman." Madison didn't want to feel left out. And it gave her an excuse to ditch the name "Lundquist" and the baggage that went with it.

Madison enrolled the three of them in Lamaze classes. She wanted to do things right. Alex had to be there, being the father, but she chose Lucy as her birth coach. Alex was supportive in a male way, but there was the kind of support that only another woman could provide. Madison felt she needed that, and Lucy was happy to provide it.

When they got home after the first Lamaze class, the new owners of the Holloway home were unloading a truck. Lucy opened the car door and called to them.

"Hey, neighbors! Welcome!"

A woman came over to the low hedges, smiling.

"I'm Lucy."

The woman extended her hand. "Ellen. Pleased to meet you."

Alex and Madison had stopped for a kiss on their way to the front door.

Lucy said, "Hey, guys! Come meet Ellen!"

Alex and Madison approached the hedge, holding hands.

"We just got back from Lamaze class," Lucy said. She looked at Alex and Madison and sighed. "They're in love. Aren't they cute?"

"You're pregnant!" Ellen said. "How far along are you?"

"Thirty weeks," Madison said. "In the home stretch, no pun intended."

"This is my friend Madison, and my husband, Alex," Lucy said.

Ellen looked confused. "I'm sorry. Your husband?"

"Yes."

"And he's the father?"

The three Hermans, in unison, said, "Yes."

Ellen's jaw dropped. She turned without saying another word and practically ran into the house.

"I can see she's going to be a challenge," Lucy said.

She made a mental note: she would have to be more careful with her introductions.

•❤•❤•❤•❤•❤•

Lucy started teaching Madison how to cook. Madison discovered that she had potential. They were confident that she would improve.

One day, Madison said, "What about Alex?"

"What do you mean?" Lucy asked.

"Would it kill him if he learned to cook?"

Lucy laughed. She didn't think it would. She persuaded Alex to join them for lessons, and he, too, proved to be adequate.

They divided the household chores, giving Lucy plenty of time to paint. She wondered why she had ever stopped.

Madison told Lucy it was okay for Lucy and Alex to be physically intimate if they ever felt the urge. After all, Lucy was still Alex's legal wife.

"No thanks," said Lucy. "That ship has sailed." As for intimacy with Alex, Lucy would be satisfied with the occasional hug or a kiss on the forehead.

Madison was secretly relieved to hear that.

The three of them did sleep together sometimes. The first time was an accident. They had been watching a movie in the master bedroom on the king-sized bed, Madison on one side, Lucy on the other, and Alex between them. They fell asleep in the middle of the movie. Alex felt awkward when he woke in the morning, but it had been innocent. The women acted as if nothing unusual had happened. It happened again, then again, and eventually became a Saturday night tradition. They didn't have to follow anyone else's rules.

Lucy threw a baby shower in April when Madison was seven months along. Tucker-Herman staff attended, along with Madison's sister Colleen. They ate from an interesting buffet that Lucy put together and had cake. They opened gifts for the mom and the coming baby and played video games. Everyone, except for Madison and Alex, drank wine and beer. They toasted the unusual family.

Lilith performed a commitment ceremony. She wasn't ordained, but she was qualified enough, being the high priestess of her Neo-Pagan worship group. Credentials didn't matter anyway because the ceremony had no legal standing—it was just a chance for Alex and Madison to declare their love in front of family and friends.

When the time came, Lilith donned a beautiful white robe with gold trim. Here are some of the things she said:

"Love is intertwined with life and takes many forms. Its reasons are infinite. Among these are to bring forth life; to support life; and to give life meaning, making it worth living.

"When two people come together in love, in body, mind, and soul, it can only be described as holy, whatever the circumstances. It is up to us to nurture and support that love.

"Answer together: will you, Alex and Madison, support and nurture this love, the only bond that binds you?"

Alex and Madison said, "We will."

Lilith addressed the witnesses: "Will you, family and friends, support and nurture this love?"

Everyone said, "We will."

"And now, with absolutely no power vested in me by the state, I pronounce you husband and wife. You may kiss, now and whenever you wish, forever."

Alex and Madison kissed. Everyone applauded.

It was beautiful. Lucy cried a little. So did Bob.

Lilith had placed a figurine of a woman in the corner of the room while preparing for the ceremony. It reminded Lucy of someone. She asked Lilith about it afterward.

"That's a replica of a Mediterranean love deity," Lilith said. "From around the time of The Bronze Age Collapse. I thought she'd like to be here."

"Kori tis Thalassis?" Lucy asked.

Lilith seemed surprised. "Yes. Probably an earlier name for Aphrodite." That made Lucy smile. "You know her?"

"I do," Lucy said.

Colleen had finally gotten to see what was East of Chicago. She returned to Wisconsin confident that her sister was loved and supported.

Lucy missed Kay, who was busy with her "new adventure" in Maui. Lucy was sad at times, but she had memories to console her and a future to look forward to.

It was time to move on. Lucy joined an online dating site designed for women. She found a match and arranged a date for the Saturday night before Madison was due.

She was anxious, so she asked the others if they would go with her in a show of support. They were happy to go along.

She wore that sexy blue dress Kay had bought the night they had gone dancing.

Lucy was meeting her date for dinner. The Hermans were seated at a circular booth, with Lucy sitting opposite Alex, facing the door. Hannah sat next to her mother, and Madison sat next to Alex.

Their server came and offered a wine list.

"Let's see," Alex said. "I'm in recovery. She's pregnant," pointing at Madison, "she's a minor," pointing at Hannah. "Lucy?"

"I'll abstain in solidarity," she said.

"Water for everyone," said Alex.

"I'm so nervous!" said Lucy.

"You'll be fine," Madison said.

"Thanks for coming along. It means a lot. I don't think I could do this by myself."

"This is what families do," Madison said.

A woman walked through the door. Lucy compared her to the photo on her phone.

"There she is. Here goes."

She rose to greet the woman.

"She's beautiful," Madison said.

They watched as Lucy introduced herself. She pointed to their booth and brought the woman back for introductions.

"Everyone, this is Rebecca. Rebecca, this is my family. My husband Alex..." He rose and shook Rebecca's hand. "Our daughter Hannah...and Alex's... girlfriend? Madison."

Madison extended her hand. "I prefer the term 'mistress.'"

"Yep! She's pregnant!" Lucy blurted. Her anxiety was making her talkative.

Rebecca smiled. "I think it's wonderful. When are you due?" she asked Madison.

"Any day now."

"Congratulations! Alex, I've got a table on the other side of the room. I'd like to borrow your wife so we can get to know each other." It sounded as if she was asking permission.

"That's why we're here," he said.

Rebecca led Lucy away. Lucy looked back at Alex. He crossed his fingers and held them up for her to see.

"I've got a good feeling about this," Alex said.

"Me, too," Madison said.

She felt a spasm in her belly before their salads came. She didn't say anything—it was the first. She figured it was a Braxton-Hix contraction.

The second contraction came as she took the first bite of her steak. It made her wince.

"What's the matter?" Alex asked.

"Contraction."

"First one?"

"Second."

"How far apart?"

She looked at her watch. "Twenty minutes." The next contraction came right away. She groaned. "Oh! Baby's not playin'!"

"We've got to go!" Alex said. He panicked. He tried to flag the waitress. "No time!" He pulled his wallet out and threw some bills onto the table. "Hannah, get the car." He handed her his keys. Hannah flew to the door. He helped Madison to her feet.

Lucy saw the commotion from across the room.

"Oh! Oh!" she said. "It's happening!" She got to her feet. Her arms flapped wildly. Her date turned to see Alex helping Madison to the door.

"I'm sorry," Lucy said. "I have to go. I'm her birth coach."

"Which hospital?"

"University."

"I'll have them box the food. I'll meet you there."

That was unexpected and kind, coming from a stranger. Lucy touched Rebecca's hand. "Thank you."

She turned and ran after Alex and Madison. She couldn't contain herself.

"Ahhhhh!" she said, waving her arms excitedly.

They had time in the waiting room as the team prepped Madison for the delivery. Lucy sat next to Rebecca, nibbling from take-out boxes.

Lucy was able to calm herself. Everything was in the hands of Fate and the obstetrician.

Alex and Hannah sat together on the sofa across from her. Lucy's heart was practically bursting with love for them.

Her sweet Hannah was finally getting a baby brother.

And Alex, her friend, her soulmate—the smallest things could turn him into a quivering ball of nerves, but at times like this, when it counted, he was solid as a rock. She had married well, with no regrets, despite everything. Alex was happy, and that made her happy. Life was good.

And Rebecca? Maybe it would work out, and maybe it wouldn't. It was too early to tell. But the woman had kind eyes. Lucy was optimistic.

Rebecca smiled and said, "Interesting first date." Implying there would be more to come.

"Yeah, a little *too*."

A nurse came into the waiting room. It was showtime.

"Dad? Coach?" the nurse said. Alex and Lucy stood. "She's ready," the nurse said. "She's asking for you."

Alex took Lucy's hand. They smiled at each other and walked to the delivery room side by side.

A wave of bliss washed over Lucy.

She didn't know what the future would look like, but she had a feeling it would be strange and beautiful.

THE END

About the Author

JP McAndrew studied writing at Eastern Michigan University. He focused on screenplays and dramatic writing. Writing novels is a new experience for him. He dabbles in music, video, and martial arts. He is a practicing Zen Baptist.He lives in corn country south of Ann Arbor, Michigan, with two rescue dogs, a cat, and his soulmate Kimberly.

Dear reader,

If you enjoyed this story, please let other people know. You can share your feelings on social media, leave a review on Amazon (or whichever platform you purchased it from), and tell the people in your life. Nothing promotes a book as well as word-of-mouth and personal endorsements. It's so important to indie authors.

The author can be reached through email at: jpmcandrew039@gmail.com.

If you'd like a live appearance at a bookstore or library, just ask. We can probably make that happen.

And stay tuned for the further adventures of Kay, Daughter of the Sea.

www.ingramcontent.com/pod-product-compliance
Lightning Source LLC
LaVergne TN
LVHW100521110826
845146LV00002B/735

* 9 7 9 8 2 1 8 2 4 3 1 0 4 *